Phoebe continued to speak in that unnaturally calm manner, and every sentence was more fantastic than the one before. "The last time," she said, "you insisted that I fulfill my duty as a wife. Now it is only fair that you should fulfill your duty as my husband." She sounded like a governess lecturing a recalcitrant pupil. "You may as well resign yourself to making love to me, Charles, for I shall not leave this house until you do."

It was

= *The Marplot Marriage* =

The Marplot Marriage

by

Beth Andrews

Regency Press
Cleveland Heights, Ohio

THE MARPLOT MARRIAGE

Regency Press is a division of
Crack of Noon Enterprises, Incorporated.
The name Regency Press and the Crowned R are registered trademarks of Crack of Noon Enterprises, Incorporated.

ISBN: 1-929085-01-x

First Edition: October, 1999

Printed in the United States of America

0 9 8 7 6 5 4 3 2 1

In memory of
my father,
Wayne Bethel

***Dad,
I'm sorry you can't be here
to share this with me.
I couldn't have done it
without you!***

Chapter One

England, 1817

"Would you be so good as to inform me, ma'am, what you are doing in my bed?"

Phoebe, staring over the covers in mute horror at the man beside her, was quite incapable of providing the requested information. Indeed, she was more than half inclined to believe that this entire episode was nothing more than a very bad dream. Had she been so absolutely abandoned as to crawl into bed with a man, Charles Hargood would certainly not be the man she would choose. It was too ridiculous! Surely, when she awoke, this would all be no more than a somewhat laughable memory.

She was just about to turn over and return to sleep when she paused uneasily. The stiff, accusing countenance of her reluctant bed partner certainly seemed real enough. She had never imagined Mr. Hargood being in bed with any woman; but had she made the attempt, she felt that it would be just like the man to wear that absurdly pompous look on his face. Very well, then. This was no illusion.

In all fairness, she supposed that she ought to answer his question—though she hardly knew what explanation she might reasonably make. As if her surroundings might provide inspiration, she looked around her, distractedly. She then perceived, much to her satisfaction, that it was she who had every right to be offended. Giving him a look of haughty disdain—a wonderful achievement for a woman in her situation—she addressed him in icy tones. "I believe, sir, that it is I who should be inquiring as to what you are doing in my bed!"

This was too much for Charles Hargood. Phoebe Bridgerton was a wild, hoydenish, unprincipled baggage. He had always thought so and had made no secret of his objection to her marriage with his cousin, Robert. In all conscience, Charles had to admit she was a lovely piece. But no man of sense would wish to be leg-shackled to such a shatter-brained little flirt. Had Robert not died of a perfectly respectable fever, Charles would have sworn that his wife's antics had driven him to a premature grave.

How he came to be sharing a bed with the wench was quite beyond him. It could hardly be by design, for her contempt of him was as well known as was his antipathy toward her.

When he awakened to find his arm resting comfortably around her very shapely form, he had thought for a startled moment that he must be quite mad. What had happened here last night?

He would never willingly have taken this woman to his bed.

Therefore, it must be her doing. But what could have possessed her? Was it some devious scheme to embarrass him?

Surely even she would not go so far.

"I am waiting for your explanation, ma'am," he insisted stubbornly.

Phoebe sat bolt upright in bed at this effrontery. Unfortunately, she forgot to secure the bedcovers, which promptly fell to her waist, revealing a very fetching linen nightgown.

Shocked at such a vulgar display, and quite forgetting that he was in an even greater state of undress, Charles quickly averted his eyes until she could cover herself. If only he could have as easily averted his thoughts! But these traitors continued to return to that all-too-brief glimpse of feminine beauty, and he was much annoyed to find himself wondering what it would be like to hold such a delectable bundle—

"How dare you?" Her magnificent green eyes blazing, Phoebe sat bolt upright in bed, hauling the covers up to her chin. "Am I not the injured party here?"

Self-disgust at his unexpected response to her made Charles's voice even sharper than usual. "May I remind you that you are in my home," he said. "And this, as it happens, is my bedchamber!"

Of course! Phoebe wondered how she could have been so foolish. The solid oak furniture, the dull green draperies at bed and windows, were quite distinctive. She was forced to admit that this odious man was right for once.

"Yes," she said, hating the necessity of having to agree with him. "Your mother explained as much yesterday. Since the house was quite full up with guests, however, there was nowhere else for me until another chamber could be prepared. But," she added accusingly, "you were not supposed to return home until tomorrow!"

"Well, I did not. I arrived last night."

"So I perceive. And promptly got into my bed!"

"It is *my* bed," he corrected her, glowering. "And believe me, ma'am, had I been aware of your presence here, I would have been happy to find an excuse to remain in town. I certainly would not have come near this room—much less the bed."

"I am well aware of your feelings for me," Phoebe said, unaccountably piqued by his obvious repugnance. "Allow me to say that they exactly match mine for you! Still, I do not see how you could have failed to discover that your bed was already occupied—unless you were foxed."

"I have never been inebriated in my entire

life."

"More's the pity," she returned tartly.

He glared at her in silence, his too-firm jaw set and a vein pulsing in his throat as though his temper was perilously close to snapping. For the first time Phoebe noticed, with something like shock, that his bare chest was very broad and muscled, covered with a thick mat of silky dark hair.

The only other man with whom she had ever been this intimate had been her husband, but Robert's body had been almost as smooth as her own. She had a strong suspicion that Charles was as bare beneath the covers as he was above them. What would it be like, she wondered, to touch—

"I left London earlier than I intended," Charles's voice interrupted these appalling thoughts, "but the carriage wheel broke during the journey, and I did not arrive here until well after midnight. No one was about but Simpson, whom I dismissed. I was quite exhausted," he explained, "and only waited for a quick wash before I came to my room, removed my clothes and got into bed. I was asleep almost before my head touched the pillow."

"And you were conscious of nothing unusual?" Phoebe was incredulous. Could he really have been unaware of her presence? But he would hardly have got into bed with her deliberately—would he? She was no longer sure. Indeed, she was not sure about anything, least of all her own emotions.

Charles was attempting to give a reasonable account of his actions. "I had only the light of a single taper to see by," he said. "And I suppose I must have been too tired to notice much of anything. I might ask how you did not come to hear me or to feel my weight in the bed beside you?"

"I have always been a sound sleeper," she admitted ruefully. "Until today it did not seem to be of any great significance."

"Do you realize the position in which you have placed me?" Charles demanded. "If Olivia should hear of this—"

Phoebe could scarcely credit this utter insensibility. "Your position!" she cried, her temper flaring. "Can you think of nobody but yourself? You have nothing to fear! Your simpering Olivia will forgive and forget. Your friends will wink knowingly at you and call you a sly fox—and that will be an end to it! But if anyone should learn of this, my reputation would be ruined. Only men have the privilege of making such mistakes."

She compressed her lips, suppressing the urge to use even stronger language. "It would be useless, of course, to claim that nothing happened. Who would believe us? Or, if they did, it were almost worse! We should appear such fools. And I had as lief be a loose woman as a laughing stock!"

Despite her disparaging reference to his betrothed, Charles could not deny that there was some degree of truth to Phoebe's remarks. This prompted him to say, rather more gently, "Well, we are being a little premature. If I can contrive to leave here unnoticed, we may yet be able to avoid a scandal. After all, no one knows about this unfortunate accident."

This very sensible observation had barely escaped his lips, however, when the door of the bedchamber flew open to admit a charmingly attired young lady who was already launched into impetuous speech.

"Phoebe, I have the most wonderful—" Letitia Comston's breathless words halted abruptly at the unexpected sight which met her eyes. Then she permitted herself the luxury of a very effective and quite ear-shattering shriek, before fainting dead away.

Fortunately—or, in this instance it might be considered more of a misfortune—Letitia did not actually disgrace herself by collapsing upon the floor in an ungainly heap. Instead, she was caught in the arms of the maid, Gladys, who had rushed in behind her at the sound of her scream.

"Gawd 'elp us!" Gladys exclaimed, supporting Letitia and goggling at the very same sight which had just rendered that limp damsel unconscious. A plain, stout-hearted country girl, Gladys knew nothing of fainting. So she continued to stare at the spectacle in the bed.

"We are certainly in the basket now, Charles!" Phoebe said fatalistically.

Pleased to see that she was not so chicken-hearted as to emulate her fainting friend, Charles preserved a stolid countenance. But even his self-control was taxed to the limit a moment later when Miss Olivia Loftbury and her formidable mama materialized in the still open doorway.

It was a scene which would have been a tremendous success at Drury Lane. Charles could almost picture Mrs. Siddons and Mr. Kean in place of Phoebe and himself. In real life, however, it was not nearly so amusing.

"Charles!" Miss Loftbury gasped. Her face, so like the horses which she loved, was wooden with shock.

"Olivia, I can explain," Charles began desperately. "This is not what it appears, believe me. Phoebe means nothing to me! You, of all people, should know that."

At this moment the spirit of mischief, which some believed to be Phoebe's besetting sin, totally overcame her common sense.

Realizing only that she was being presented with a golden opportunity to give the odious Charles a leveler from which he would not easily recover, she said outrageously, "Oh, Charles! You heartless wretch to trifle with me so! When you swore to love me forever!"

At these impassioned words, a martial light appeared in Mrs. Loftbury's bulging eyes. Her ample bosom heaving with ill-suppressed wrath, she prepared to fire a volley at poor Charles, who was already reeling from Phoebe's assault.

"Philanderer!" Mrs. Loftbury cried. "Libertine! Vile seducer—" Running out of epithets, she began to sputter.

"Rake?" Phoebe suggested helpfully. "Viper? Scurvy knave? Hypocrite?"

"Be quiet!" Charles snapped, not at all appreciating the ill-timed mirth he recognized in her sparkling eyes. The wench was enjoying this! It would serve her right if he boxed her ears. If he could only stand and face his accusers with some measure of dignity; but in his present state of undress, that was out of the question.

"Mrs. Loftbury," he said in a futile attempt to retrieve a position which grew ever more hopeless, "I have always preserved a spotless reputation. My conduct, as you know, has ever been above reproach—"

Miss Loftbury, rearing up in obvious indignation, cut short this ever-so-pious defense. "How can you, Charles?" she said. "Here you are, in bed with Phoebe, acting no more concerned than if you were having a cup of tea. I dare swear it is not the first time that you have enjoyed her—her favors! No doubt your previous contempt for each other was merely a pose assumed to cover your shameful affair from the eyes of the world!"

"Do not be such a fool, Olivia," her betrothed said in a distressingly unlover-like manner. "This is utter nonsense. I do not know how you can believe what you are saying."

"How can I not believe it, when I see it before my eyes this very moment?"

"Prevarication is useless now, my love. Our guilty secret is out at last," said Phoebe with a soulful glance at Charles, who would have given a great deal to throttle her there and then.

Meanwhile Letitia, whom Gladys had managed to revive with the aid of Mrs. Loftbury's hartshorn, was surveying the various actors in this farce with a look of increasing bewilderment.

"Oh," Letitia said at last, "there must be some dreadful mistake. Why, I have heard Phoebe say any number of times that Charles is the biggest bore in England and that no woman in her right mind would contemplate marrying him. I am sure she would rather die than have him for her lover."

As she seemed to be the only one present who believed the truth of the matter, Charles ought to have been grateful for her support. For some inexplicable reason, however, he found himself very much annoyed at her earnest speech and glowered at her so fiercely that she stepped back hastily and was absolutely incapable of uttering another word.

Unfortunately, Olivia's mama was not so easily silenced.

"My dear child," she cried, "it is obvious that that woman has deceived us all. Not that I ever thought so much of her myself. She always seemed very fast to me. Now I perceive that she is little better than a common harlot!"

"You go too far, ma'am!" Charles exclaimed involuntarily. Phoebe was certainly an irritating thorn in his flesh, but he had no reason to suspect her of any immorality. "You are cruel and unjust, and I cannot permit such aspersions to be cast on Mrs. Bridgerton's character. She is, after all, my mother's guest as well as the widow of my cousin Robert."

Phoebe, staring at Charles in genuine surprise, was torn between an unexpected feeling of pleasure at his spirited defense and a desire to burst out laughing at the absurdity of it in their present circumstances. Was there more to the man than met the eye? Surely not! He was the same odiously starched-up prig he had ever been.

The other occupants of the room were staring at Charles as well, with varying degrees of affront or approbation. It was Olivia who eventually broke the silence which had descended in the wake of his noble words. "I have never been so humiliated in my entire life!" she said. "That you should lie there and defend your mistress before your own fiancée and your intended mama-in-law! I shall never recover from this, Charles. Never."

Olivia swept from the room in high dudgeon, and it was left to her mother to deliver her valedictory oration.

"My daughter and I shall remove ourselves from this place at once, and I shall send a notice to the Gazette as soon as may be possible. Your engagement to my daughter is at an end, sir!" she intoned with awful finality. "I would never countenance such a connection. My regrets to your mother—and I hope never to be obliged to see your deceitful face again. Your conduct has been monstrous, and I can only take comfort from the thought that your sins have at last found you out and that you shall certainly reap what you have sown! Good day to you, sir!"

She marched out the door in solemn majesty, like an old soldier, dignified even in retreat. Her departure left yet another uncomfortable silence in the room. Charles had retreated into a brown study and seemed to have lost interest in the whole affair. Phoebe, feeling that some action was called for, decided to dismiss the still-goggling Gladys and the mutely pleading Letitia.

"Say nothing of this, either of you," she warned them, though she could hardly say why. It would be impossible to keep such a story secret for very long, especially once the news of Charles's broken engagement was out.

"But Phoebe, what...?" Letitia began, apparently seeking some assurance that her dear friend had not taken complete leave of her senses.

"Not now, Letty," Phoebe said with a look that brooked no further questions. "You had best go with Gladys. I will speak with you later. For the present, Mr. Hargood and I wish to be left alone. I am sure Charles will be glad of a little privacy in which to mourn for lost love or some such thing. And I," she added, "am hardly in any mood for company now myself."

After these last two spectators retired, closing the door reluctantly behind them, Charles spoke. "I hope that you are satisfied with this morning's work, madam."

"I declare," she said, stung by his accusing look and feeling uncomfortably guilty, "it was almost worth it all just to see the look on Olivia's face. And as for her mother! It is high time that toplofty pair were put in their place."

"There is no need for you to make disparaging remarks about Miss Loftbury or her mother. They have already suffered enough from your conduct"

"You were the one who called Olivia a fool!" Phoebe reminded him. As his only response to this was a pronounced frown, she continued more calmly. "I am sorry if I have behaved badly. The temptation was irresistible, believe me. But," she challenged him, "do you honestly think that any other behavior on my part would have made a difference? If so, then you have greater faith in human nature than I can lay claim to. The moment Miss Loftbury stepped through that door, your engagement was as good as over, for only a saint would have believed us innocent."

"Perhaps," Charles admitted. "But your actions did nothing to alleviate the situation. You have wrecked my engagement and destroyed any hope I cherished of domestic felicity."

"Stuff and nonsense! Olivia will never contribute to anyone's felicity—domestic or otherwise. Why, even her own mother is itching to be rid of her! I am only surprised that Mrs. Loftbury has broken off the engagement, for it is highly unlikely that she will ever find any other gudgeon to take Olivia off her hands."

Charles stiffened perceptibly at this, his lips compressed in a manner which showed that he did not at all appreciate Phoebe's comments. "I might have known," he said, "that you would treat this with your usual display of vulgar levity. Have you no thought for the damage you have done?"

"Really, Charles!" Phoebe said. "I am not to blame for this predicament, and well you know it. This display of temper is no more than wounded pride. It's not as if you were in love with her, after all."

"My feelings for Miss Loftbury are no concern of yours, ma'am."

"I daresay they are scarcely worth my concern. No doubt, you are as incapable of passion as you are of wit! And now," she added scornfully, "if you would kindly remove yourself, I should like to have my maid come and dress me."

Ignoring this request, he bent a hard look upon her. "I may not be Beau Brummell, ma'am, but I would advise you to accustom yourself to my lack of wit. You are going to be obliged to endure it for some time to come."

"What on earth are you talking about?"

"Are you really such a pea-goose that you cannot see the inevitable consequence of what has occurred here this morning?"

"You mean—" she began, with sudden foreboding.

"I mean, " Charles answered, his words like a barrage of stones, battering Phoebe's sensiblity, "that if either of us is to salvage even a scrap of reputation, you must marry me, my dear Phoebe—as soon as it can be decently arranged."

"Marry you?" Phoebe had the curious impression that the walls of the room had suddenly retreated to a great distance. Heaven help her! Was she now going to swoon as well? "No!" she managed to gasp. "I could never...it is quite impossible."

"On the contrary. It is now the only possible avenue open to us."

"Surely not," she pleaded. "There must be some other alternative. Anything would be preferable to—to—"

"To being my wife?"

"Yes!"

His eyes narrowed as he surveyed her flushed countenance. "Believe me, ma'am, the prospect of being your husband is quite as disagreeable to me as it is to you. But I fear we must both resign ourselves to it."

"I cannot believe that such desperate measures are required."

"Oh?"

Phoebe could not miss the sarcasm behind this simple question.

"And, as my cast-off mistress—which is certainly how you will be perceived if we do not wed—how do you think you will be looked upon by polite society? How many of your old acquaintances will give you the cut direct? Would you dare even to show your face again at Almack's? How much would you care to wager on the likelihood of your being admitted?"

"Surely nobody will believe such a thing?" she suggested hopefully.

"What else can they believe?"

"It is wicked and unjust!"

"You found it amusing enough a few minutes ago," he reminded her, "when you were making a

May-game of Olivia and her mother."

"That was different," she said in self-defense. "They deserved it."

"The only difference is that what you strove so hard to convince them of, is merely what everyone else will believe without any effort on your part." He paused before adding, with some reluctance, "It is, as you pointed out a moment ago, the most logical assumption—and what I myself would probably think of anyone else discovered in such a situation.

Confound the man. He was making sense, as usual. Why had she not stopped to consider what was to be done? Well, it appeared that she was fated to become Mrs. Charles Hargood. It was unsettling. But Phoebe was surprised to find that it did not feel as strange as she might have expected. On the other hand, with Charles lying naked in bed beside her, she wondered if anything else would ever feel strange to her again.

Chapter Two

Phoebe was amazed at her own stupidity. Making her way down to breakfast after a brief and bitter discussion with Charles, she could only marvel at herself. It had not taken her very long to see that Charles was right: marriage was the only possible solution to their deplorable dilemma—however unlikely it might be of contributing to their future happiness.

It had been determined between them that it was best to let the world believe theirs was a love match. After all, as Charles had pointed out, there would be no need for any public display of affection on either side. Such vulgar demonstrations were not at all the thing for modish members of polite society. For once in his miserable life, Charles Hargood was eager to follow fashion—a circumstance which pleased Phoebe not one bit. In fact, as she trudged toward the breakfast room, her thoughts toward Mr. Hargood were anything but cordial.

Breakfast at Camberley was always a rather haphazard affair. How Charles, who was punctual to a fault, put up with his mother's less than orderly management of his household, was a mystery to Phoebe. Though not renowned for his patience, Charles seemed capable of the most incredible feats of long-suffering where family and friends were concerned.

Charles was one of those terrible people who generally kept country hours, rising at the most ungodly time of day to break his fast. Phoebe was happy to realize that today he would be much later than usual—and serve him right, too! She herself never sat down to breakfast before eleven.

Whenever a fairly large party assembled at Camberley, there was a slow trickle of guests partaking of their meal at all hours of the morning. Certainly one was not likely to find a large number of people gathered around the polished oak table at one time. It was therefore something of a shock for Phoebe to be greeted by the sight of no less than five curious faces peering at her over forgotten ham and toast.

Obviously, this morning's debacle was already common knowledge amongst her fellow guests. She could almost hear the wheels of collective imaginations turning at breakneck pace while the diners inspected her for some outward sign of her recent depravity. Well, she could hardly turn tail and run now!

Shooting an accusing glance at Letty's anxious countenance, Phoebe stepped boldly forward. With perfect unconcern, she moved to the sideboard and proceeded to help herself to a breakfast of gargantuan proportions. She absolutely refused to let this lamentable display of curiosity disconcert her.

There was a moment of strained silence as Phoebe selected a nice piece of ham, then Mrs. Hargood said, "I—I do hope you had a—a restful night, Phoebe."

This opening gambit might well have undone anyone of lesser mettle, but once again Phoebe's irrepressible sense of humor came to her aid. "I had a most delightful evening, ma'am," she said with a wicked look as she finished filling her plate and came to sit down beside the lady. "Indeed, I do not know how I shall I stay out of Charles's bed in future! It was quite inspired of you to put me there."

At this artless pronouncement, Mrs. Hargood,

who was sipping a cup of coffee, began to choke violently. Letitia looked as if she was about to swoon again. And Sir John Northcote, at the opposite end of the table, just managed to cover his mouth with his hand while his shoulders shook suspiciously. Lady Northcote stared at Phoebe as if the poor girl had run mad. Only young Harry Northcote, a strapping lad of fifteen, remained impervious to the entire situation and continued to eat his breakfast with perfect unconcern.

"Phoebe!" Letitia cried. "For heaven's sake, what are you saying?"

"Why Letty," Phoebe said, turning toward her friend a look of the most limpid innocence, "you seem so distressed. Surely it cannot be because I spent so enjoyable a night in Charles's bedchamber?"

Charles himself, entering the room just in time to catch this pronouncement, wondered what on earth the wretched woman would do next.

He had not long to wait for the answer. The moment that Phoebe spied him, she flew from her seat with a rapturous cry of "Charles! Dearest!" While the other occupants of the room looked on in helpless fascination, she flung herself upon Mr. Hargood, wrapped her arms around his neck and kissed him soundly on the cheek.

If she had hoped to discompose him by this effusive display, she was disappointed in her design. Charles, who felt that he had more than one score to settle with this lively lady, immediately took control of the situation. Instead of swiftly disentangling himself from her clinging arms, as Phoebe had fully expected, he pulled her roughly against him and pressed a very thorough kiss upon her startled lips.

Before Phoebe had any time to recover from the shock of his unexpected response, Charles raised his head and turned to address the assembled company. He still kept one arm firmly about Phoebe's waist, which was just as well, since she was so much shaken that she felt she might have fallen without his support.

"I think it only right and fitting to inform you all," Charles began, "that Mrs. Loftbury and her daughter have chosen to curtail their visit with us. My engagement to Olivia is at an end," he added, unconsciously employing Mrs. Loftbury's phrase. "Olivia has been generous enough to release me from my obligation to her, so that I might be free to offer my hand and heart to another.

"Though I hardly dared to hope that my feelings were reciprocated, my beloved Phoebe has at last consented to become my wife. It is impossible for me to describe my emotions at this moment, but I know you may all imagine the feelings of a man who has attained his heart's desire."

Phoebe, not missing the note of irony with which this last sentence was uttered, nobly resisted the urge to box his ears. At least she had to give him credit for breaking the news with admirable coolness and brevity. His was a speech worthy of the most double-faced of politicians. It had also given her a blessed opportunity to recover her equilibrium.

She might just as well resign herself to the inevitable and play the part of blushing bride to the hilt. After all, they had both decided to present the world with a tortuous tale involving a secret attachment of long standing between them, which had been hampered by jealousy and misunderstanding, and to which Miss Loftbury's magnanimity had removed the last impediment. That anyone could possibly be deceived by such a nonsensical farrago seemed extremely unlikely to Phoebe, but she saw no reasonable alternative. She had always loved theatricals, and now that she had a leading role in this comedy of errors, she had best make the most of it.

"Is no one going to wish us joy?" she said, linking her arm with Charles's and flashing a brilliant smile upon her audience.

At once there was a babble of confused congratulations, each one attempting to outdo the other with their expressions of happiness for the unlikely couple. Charles's hand was shaken vigorously. Phoebe's cheek was kissed by the ladies amid a flurry of insincere pleasantries.

Harry alone remained seated, apparently quite uninterested in the recent revelations, until called to book by his Mama. "Harry! For goodness' sake! Where are your manners? Are you not going to congratulate Charles and Phoebe on their betrothal?"

Swallowing his last mouthful, Harry looked up, a trifle confused by this development. "Thought Charles was to marry Miss Loftbury," he said.

"That," Phoebe informed him, "was all a mistake, but one which has fortunately been remedied in time."

"Phoebe is the woman I love," Charles said stiffly, and not at all convincingly as far as Phoebe was concerned. Really, he would have to do better than that.

Harry, however, seemed to accept the whole thing as perfectly natural. "Of course," he said. "You'll be much better off with Phoebe, too. Never liked that Miss Loftbury. Silly woman. Got no more warmth than an adder."

"Master Harry approves!" Phoebe cried, a glint in her eye which perhaps only Charles recognized as unholy amusement. "What more could one ask?"

Master Harry's parents—thankful, no doubt, for Phoebe's lack of sensibility—quickly hustled their son out of the room before he could utter anything more outrageous. With their departure, Charles abruptly released Phoebe and asked his mother to have his breakfast sent to his study, where he had some urgent estate business to attend to.

"Do you desert me so soon, my dearest?" Phoebe asked, affecting a wounded look.

Her "dearest" did not appear at all pleased by her fond words. "Never fear," he said. "I shall speak with you later—my dove!"

"I live for the moment," she called after him as he marched stiffly from the room.

"Phoebe! You cannot possibly marry Charles!" Letitia exclaimed as soon as Mr. Hargood had made his exit. She had quite neglected to remember the fact that Charles's mother was standing directly behind her.

"Why not?" Mrs. Hargood asked. "I'm sure my son is good enough for anyone!"

"Certainly, ma'am," Letty agreed, attempting to repair her blunder. "But I cannot believe—that is, I do not think that he and Phoebe are at all well suited. Olivia would have been a much better wife for Charles."

"I'm afraid Harry disagrees with you, Letty." Phoebe said.

"Oh pooh! Harry is a mere child. What does he know of such matters?"

"And what do you know of such matters, come to that?" said Mrs. Hargood, obviously annoyed at Letty's interference in goings on which did not concern her. "A chit scarce out of the schoolroom!"

Letty began to protest this offensive description, but Phoebe intervened before the discussion could develop into a battle. "Any further argument on this subject will surely be a waste of breath. I am going to marry Charles," she insisted, "and that is all there is to it."

"Oh, this is terrible!"

Phoebe could not help smiling at Letty's dramatic outburst. But really, it was time that her friend learned to curb her errant tongue. Impetuosity could be a charming trait in a young woman, but there was no doubt that it palled very quickly and soon became severely irritating to the nerves.

"Do try for a little self-control, Letty," she said. "And remember your company."

Letitia subsided, momentarily abashed by this unexpected censure from her dearest friend, and began to apologize. "I meant no offense, truly. It is just so—so unexpected. You and Charles have always held each other in such aversion! I cannot understand it, indeed."

"No more can I," Mrs. Hargood said with an abrupt *volte-face*. "Not that I wouldn't be happy to have you for my daughter-in-law. After all, anyone were better than that Friday-faced Olivia!"

"Thank you," Phoebe replied, scarcely able to stifle a laugh at this charmingly back-handed compliment. "And I shall adore having you for a mama-in-law."

"Yes, but that is not the point," Mrs. Hargood said, refusing to be put off. "Letitia is right. You and Charles have never even liked each other. I remember thinking the very first time that Robert introduced you, that I had never seen a more instantaneous antipathy. You are forever quizzing Charles, and I have heard him say I know not how many times that Robert is better off in his grave than married to you."

"He says that, does he?" Phoebe asked, her eyes narrowing. "Then this is no more than poetic justice. Better off dead, indeed! Well, we shall see how *he* likes being wed to me."

Letty was wringing her hands. "But surely it is not necessary to go to such an extreme—to actually marry him!"

"Then I wish you would suggest some other expedient," Phoebe returned, folding her arms patiently. "Between yourself and Olivia," she continued, seeing that Letty offered no answer, "you may be sure that all London will very soon be acquainted with the particulars of this morning's incident. Whatever our feelings may be, Charles and I have little choice."

"If you do not care for Charles, nor he for you," Mrs. Hargood said, as if trying to puzzle something out, "then why were the two of you in bed together?"

"Yes, you have yet to explain that!" Letty added, still smarting from Phoebe's allusion to her loose tongue.

"If you mean to split hairs, Letty," Phoebe quizzed her, "I could as easily ask what brought you to my chamber at such an hour of the morning?"

For a moment, the younger girl looked blank. "Oh!" she cried. "I had quite forgotten. I had been up half the night trying to decide how I should dress when we go to Almack's next month. I finally thought of the perfect gown, and just how I wanted to arrange my hair, and I could not wait to tell you about it."

"I could surely have waited to hear it, however." Phoebe shook her head. "It's interesting to ponder on what trifling matters one's fate may hinge."

"That is all very well." Mrs. Hargood was not interested in philosophy. "But it still does not answer my question."

Phoebe sighed heavily. "As you must be well aware, it was all a terrible mistake—a mistake for which Charles and I must both pay. It was you who gave me your son's bedchamber for the night."

"But there was a large party here," Mrs. Hargood said. "There really was no other chamber as suitable. And Charles was not supposed to return until this evening!"

"Do not be upsetting yourself, ma'am," Phoebe attempted to soothe the other woman's distress. "You could not have guessed that Charles would return earlier than expected, nor that he would go directly to bed and fall fast asleep—as unaware of my presence as I was of his!"

There was an appreciable pause after this, each of her listeners trying to comprehend the incomprehensible.

"My dear Phoebe," Mrs. Hargood said at last, "if I did not know you so well—and did I not trust my own son—I would be strongly inclined to think that you had invented this whole story. You may be sure that no one else will ever believe such an outrageous tale!"

Phoebe quietly seated herself once more in her chair. "Then it is as well," she said, "that we do not mean to tell anyone else. Though you two may know the truth, the rest of the world will be presented with the charming fable of long-lost love which Charles and I have concocted between us."

"I vow, I could believe that much more readily after seeing him kiss you this morning!" Mrs. Hargood chuckled at the memory. "I declare, I was never more surprised. It is so unlike Charles!"

Mrs. Hargood had not been the only one surprised by that famous kiss. Phoebe, recalling it now, was annoyed to find herself blushing furiously. Until that moment, she would have sworn to anyone—and probably had—that Charles Hargood would not know how to kiss a woman if he tried. She was now forced to concede that this was definitely not the case. Not only did Charles know how to kiss, but it was apparent to Phoebe that he was a little too well versed in that particular art.

The conniving hypocrite! Him, with the priggish airs and insufferably spotless reputation. And all the time he had probably been kissing scores of women! Had probably shared their beds too, if the truth were known. Sluts! She found herself wondering just how many women he had kissed. Who were they? Had they enjoyed his kisses as much as…

"Charles kissed me," she said, putting a halt to emotions threatening to her peace of mind, "merely to punish me for my behavior. I'm sorry to say that I probably deserved it. There's nothing I enjoy better than plaguing him."

"Then you should be very happy as his wife," Mrs. Hargood said, giving Phoebe an unexpectedly fervent hug. "Marriage will give you ample opportunity to plague my son. I have a feeling you will do very well together, after all. Now," she added pensively, "I must go and see what I can do about arranging another room for you at once. I suppose you had better have Olivia's. That seems most appropriate."

She left the two younger women alone, apparently quite reconciled to her son's exchange of brides.

Letitia, though, was not so easily satisfied. "It seems so melancholy," she said. "You are not so very old, you know, Phoebe—only six-and-twenty. I had hoped that you would find someone dashing like Robert, and fall in love again."

This reference to Phoebe's late husband had a sobering effect. Looking out the window at the bleak February landscape, Phoebe was struck by a sudden vivid image of the tall, blond Corinthian who had swept her off her feet in her first unforgettable London season. He had been the *ton's* most eligible bachelor and she the loveliest and most sought-after of young women. Though Phoebe's family might not be wealthy or titled, they were very well-connected. How romantic it had been—how giddy and silly and wonderful! Everyone had thought them a perfect match, even the highest sticklers approving of Robert's alliance with a penniless nobody. Phoebe had believed in that fairy tale herself once.

"Robert is dead," Phoebe said, her eyes still fixed on the window. "As for me, I have put my romantic dreams behind me. Perhaps marriage to Charles will be better for me than a love match. At least we have no illusions about each other."

"How can you speak like that?" Letitia's romantic soul was obviously scandalized. "You're starting to sound like—like Charles! I almost believe you deserve each other!"

On this venomous note, she flounced from the room, leaving Phoebe to eat a cold breakfast in silent solitude.

~/~

Charles would have been grateful for a similar period of solitude himself, but he was denied any such luxury. Scarcely had he seated himself at his desk and begun to sort his receipts when there was a rap at the door announcing the arrival of his long overdue breakfast.

He was not an advocate of large meals early in the day, believing that they were ruinous to the constitution. In this case, a cup of coffee, a slice of toast with marmalade and one boiled egg were more than sufficient. In fact, so distracted was Mr. Hargood that he probably would not have noticed if the egg was raw and the toast blacker than his riding boots.

The world, at least his world, had turned upside-down overnight. When he had gone to bed the previous evening, he could not have imagined that he would awaken to find his entire future changed. And all because of that blasted woman. Could he really be contemplating marriage to such a creature?

Charles was attempting to make some sense of this impossible situation, to discover some positive aspect on which to dwell, when he was interrupted for the second time. On this occasion the intruder was his friend and nearest neighbor, Stephen Dodd. The local squire, a few years older than Charles, had yet a strong reliance on the younger man's judgment and his ability to manage a country estate.

"Good morning, Charles," the squire said cheerfully.

"'Morning, Stephen," Charles answered. "Is there some problem with the new tenant?" he asked, wondering if he had guessed the reason for his friend's visit.

"Nothing very important," Stephen said, adding a little diffidently, "It seems that congratulations are in order."

"What?"

"I met your mother in the hall—"

Charles emitted a heartfelt groan. "Say no more. I'll wager she could not restrain herself from informing you of the happy news!"

"No, indeed," Stephen said with a grin. "She was most pleased to acquaint me with it."

Charles motioned for his friend to sit down. "It will be a nine days' wonder, I'm sure," he said bitterly.

"It is a trifle…unexpected," Stephen admitted.

"I dare say. Yesterday I was betrothed to Miss Loftbury, as all the country knew. Today I am to marry—of all people—Phoebe Bridgerton! It will be wonderful if they do not cart me off to Bedlam!"

Stephen laughed outright. "That's doing it much too brown, Charles! Such things have been known to happen before."

Charles closed his eyes in painful denial. "Not to me," he said.

"That is true," his friend agreed. "But perhaps it is time that they did."

"How do you mean?"

Squire Dodd gave his friend a level look which intimated words of wisdom were to follow. "You were always a rather shy, serious young man, Charles. Your father's untimely death left you to manage your household at an early age, which only encouraged your natural taciturnity. You need to be a little less conscientious, my friend. You need to begin to enjoy life."

"I was certainly never one to cut a dash," Charles said woodenly. "That sort of behavior I left to my cousin Robert."

"And see the result," Stephen said, as if Charles had just proved his point. "Robert married Phoebe while you had to settle for Olivia Loftbury."

"You did not approve of my planned marriage to Miss Loftbury?" Charles said, scarcely able to credit what he was hearing.

Stephen shrugged ever so slightly. "Naturally I could not say anything against the lady while you were still betrothed, but I'm afraid that I cannot like Miss Loftbury. I'll tell you something else too: your mother was not very partial to her either. Believe me, Charles, you underrate your worth if you think you deserved no better than that supercilious goosecap."

"And do you honestly believe that Phoebe would be a more suitable wife for me? Can you approve of this match?"

"And can you," his friend asked with a penetrating look, "honestly tell me something, Charles? Where Miss Loftbury is concerned, was your heart ever involved? Were you ever in love with her?"

Charles hardly knew how to reply to the

squire's unorthodox question. Really, if Stephen were not such a good friend, Charles would be tempted to tell him to go to the devil. After a small pause to collect his thoughts, Charles found himself saying, "Olivia and I are far too sensible to allow callow emotions to influence such important decisions as those of matrimony. Our—arrangement—was eminently practical."

"Well," Stephen said with equal practicality, "if you merely required a young lady to take to wife, it can hardly matter to you which young lady you get."

Unable to contain his agitation, Charles stood up abruptly. "I would be content to wed almost any woman in England, including the lowest scullery maid. But not Phoebe Bridgerton!"

"Do you really dislike her so much?"

At this question, Charles was seized by a frighteningly lucid image of the kiss which he had given Phoebe such a short time ago. He truly had meant only to stop her mouth and serve her with a little of her own sauce. Dammit all! He wasn't supposed to enjoy it! But her lips had been so soft, and she had felt so very good to hold, that for a mad moment he had actually forgotten whom he was kissing and why. It had been a considerable effort to end that kiss—and had they been alone, only God knew what might have happened.

"Phoebe and I can hardly speak three words together without quarreling," Charles returned. "She is a shrewish, vixenish baggage—and I believe her opinion of me is equally well known."

Stephen's lips twitched noticeably at this. "You are certainly in the minority on this issue, old friend. There are very few men who would object to as beautiful a woman as Phoebe Bridgerton."

"Beauty is not everything," Charles said. "A pleasant nature is far more important in a woman—especially when one plans to spend the rest of one's life with her."

"Agreed," the squire said, settling himself more comfortably in his chair. "But Olivia is not the most good-natured woman I ever met. Phoebe, on the other hand, is far from being unpleasant."

"She is seldom pleasant to me."

Stephen chuckled softly to himself. "I think you have both of you enjoyed your quarrels so much that neither can bear to see them end."

Charles gave a sharp laugh, devoid of humor. "There is little likelihood of that." he declared. "I fear we are the most ill-matched pair in England."

"On one point, at least, you are both in agreement—you cannot endure each other."

"I am glad that you find our situation so amusing," Charles said drily.

"I think you are both amazingly thick-headed. But there is none so blind as he, or she, who will not see."

"What I see is a very uncomfortable future ahead with that devil's daughter. But marry her I must."

Charles could not mistake the twinkle in his friend's eye as the Squire replied, "Since it seems that you will have to live the rest of your life with her, then you had better learn to appreciate this shrew of yours, Charles."

Chapter Three

With the remainder of their guests gone, and only the faithful Letitia for company, Charles could appreciate that things must be rather dull for Phoebe. But need she amuse herself by attempting to rile him? Even his own mother, in whose upstairs sitting room they were all gathered, did not seem to notice her constant teasing. Phoebe was up to her old tricks again, quizzing him with her idiotic quotations.

"'If it were done when 'tis done, then 'twere well it were done quickly!'" she cried.

Letty was looking decidedly confused, while his mother only smiled indulgently.

"Are you contemplating murder, ma'am?" Charles inquired, correctly reading the context.

Phoebe treated him to a very grave look, which did not deceive him for a moment. "No," she said sadly. "Marriage. But I never realized before how closely related the two are."

"In our case, one may very likely lead to the other."

"How can you say so, sir?" Phoebe cried. "Are we not a pair of star-crossed lovers, united after much heartache and innumerable vicissitudes?"

"You do not really mean to try and convince everybody that this is a love match?" Letty asked for the hundredth time. "Nobody will ever believe you."

"Well, we must do our best to gammon as many people as we can," Phoebe answered. "The only alternative is to claim that we were both drunk. That explanation does have a certain appeal. But where Charles is concerned," she added, shooting an oblique glance at that gentleman, "it is almost as impossible to imagine him in his cups as it is to envision him in the throes of passion."

Charles accorded this no more than a snort indicative of his utmost contempt.

"Why not simply tell the truth?" Letty asked, obviously unable to understand the need for this subterfuge.

"My poor simpleton," Phoebe replied pityingly. "How many times must I explain to you that it would not serve? The public will always prefer a plausible lie to the truth."

"It is difficult to imagine how any man could be in bed with a woman of Phoebe's beauty and do absolutely nothing about it," Mrs. Hargood broke in, with a ridiculously disappointed look at her son.

"May I remind you that I was not even aware of Phoebe's presence," Charles returned, conscious that his face had grown uncomfortably warm.

"Otherwise, we must infer, he would have done something about it," Phoebe said with deliberate provocation. "I wonder just what that would have been?"

What Charles might have replied to this sally, Phoebe was never to learn. At that moment, Letty, who was standing beside the window looking out over the front lawn, announced suddenly, "There's a carriage coming up the drive!"

This occurrence was unusual enough to draw them all to the window, their previous discussion temporarily forgotten.

"Who is it?" Letty asked, agog with curiosity.

"We are not expecting anyone, are we?" Mrs. Hargood inquired of no one in particular.

There was a moment of silent uncertainty as four pairs of eyes strained to find some clue to the identity of the mysterious vehicle and its occupant. It was Charles himself who exclaimed at last, "Good God! Aunt Charlotte!"

"Heaven help us!" His mother looked as if she was about to have a spasm.

"And who," Phoebe asked as the carriage passed directly beneath the window, "is Aunt Charlotte?"

"A stiff-rumped old harridan," Charles replied.

"The most annoying gabble-monger I have ever known," Mrs. Hargood added. "She is quite an eccentric, almost never leaves her house in the village—unless there is some trouble in the family. She seems to consider herself the guardian of the family honor, although she is only a distant relation."

"Much as one hates to admit the connection," Charles said.

"I cannot face her." Mrs. Hargood looked helpless and more than a little frightened. "Depend upon it, she has heard of your betrothal to Phoebe and has come to quiz me about it. She will find fault with everything, lay all the blame at my door, and then go and relate every detail to her odious friends."

Though not at all eager to face the old woman himself, Charles was never one to avoid life's realities, however unpleasant. "Since there is no hope of escaping her," he said stoutly, "we must face her together. I will do my best to support you through the ordeal. Phoebe had better come, too. Aunt Charlotte will doubtless demand to see her."

"I will be there directly, Charles," Phoebe said meekly. "But if I am to face this dragon, I must make myself look presentable."

There was something decidedly suspicious about Phoebe's unnaturally demure air, Charles thought. "I see nothing wrong with your appearance," he replied.

"Flatterer," she said, smiling. "But do not worry. Letty will help me, and we shall both be down in a trice. Go along now. You do not want to keep Aunt Charlotte waiting."

As soon as the door closed behind Charles and his mother, Phoebe turned to Letty. "My dear, I have just conceived the most wicked plan imaginable. If Aunt Charlotte wants scandal-broth, she shall have her fill of it today!"

"What are you going to do?" Letty asked, her eyes round and glowing with anticipation.

"Do you go to my chamber and fetch a pillow and that blue gown—the one that wants hemming. Now hurry!"

While Letty went in search of these articles, Phoebe rummaged through her hostess's wardrobe until she had unearthed a strip of blue cloth which had originally been used for a turban.

"Is this what you wanted?" Letty asked, returning with her arms full.

"Perfect!" Phoebe replied, her eyes flashing. "Now to work!"

It was some twenty minutes before the two young women descended the wooden staircase to the hall below. There they were met by Simpson, the butler. He gave them one astonished glance before turning and tottering off to the kitchen, where it required something stronger than tea to restore his shattered nerves.

The two conspirators continued across the hall in silence, stopping outside the drawing room door. Phoebe then pressed her ear against it, the better to hear what was being said on the other side. "I was never so shocked in all my life," a strange voice, obviously Aunt Charlotte's, was saying. "You and Miss Loftbury seemed so ideally suited. Is not this Phoebe chit a widow?"

"Phoebe is Cousin Robert's widow," Charles acknowledged. "A woman of birth, beauty, and superior intellect."

"That's coming it a bit strong," Phoebe muttered, continuing to eavesdrop shamelessly.

"I hope you have not let a pretty face turn your head at your age, Charles. What are you? Four-and-thirty? Well, you ought to know what you are doing by now. You always used to be a sensible enough fellow."

"I think," Mrs. Hargood put in with quiet assurance, "that Charles has made an excellent choice. Phoebe will make him happy, I'm sure of it."

"And when is the wedding?"

"Early next month," Charles said.

"So soon?" Phoebe could well imagine the sharp look in Aunt Charlotte's eyes as she scented fresh scandal. "You're in a mighty hurry to get leg-shackled, ain't you? There's no—special—reason for this urgency, is there?"

If ever there was a perfect moment to make an entrance, this was it. Throwing open the door, Phoebe sailed into the room, Letitia in her wake.

Her sudden appearance had a stunning affect on the trio before her. Mrs. Hargood's jaw dropped several inches, pulling her mouth down into a long O of astonishment. Charles, standing beside his mother, gave a remarkably fine imitation of a marble statue. And Aunt Charlotte, her hand clutching at her chest, fell back in her chair as though about to breathe her last.

To all this, Phoebe appeared sublimely unconscious. The pillow tied round her waist making a grotesque protrusion beneath her blue gown, she waddled boldly up to Aunt Charlotte.

Looking the bacon-faced old lady in the eye, she extended her hand and made the prettiest speech. "You must be Aunt Charlotte. How d'you do? I know Charles thinks I shouldn't be receiving visitors in my present condition, but I felt I could not let you leave without first paying my respects.

"I do so adore the name Charlotte," Phoebe rattled on. "So like the dear Princess! And then, too, it reminds me of my dear Charles. If we have a daughter, we simply must call her Charlotte!"

"This," Charles explained to his aunt, who continued to stare at the stomach before her in horrified fascination, "is Phoebe."

"I can scarcely credit my own eyes," Aunt Charlotte cried, recovering at last. "Now I understand your haste to marry the girl! Thank God, you have enough decency to prevent your child from being born the wrong side of the blanket."

This forthright statement did not win much favor from her nephew, who replied, "I fear, my dear aunt, that you are laboring under a grave misapprehension."

"I must say," his aunt continued, deaf to his protest, "I would not have expected such behavior from you, Charles. Never thought you was in the petticoat line. But at least you are man enough to shoulder your responsibilities rather than shirk them."

"I will not be held responsible for—for *that*!" Charles said, indicating Phoebe's stomach with a sweep of the hand.

"How can you, sir!" Aunt Charlotte was outraged. "To deny your own child! Shameful."

But Mr. Hargood received support from an unexpected quarter. "Now, Aunt Charlotte," Phoebe said. "You must not blame poor Charles. I cannot have you laying my sins at his door. He is an innocent man, believe me. This was not his doing."

"You—you dare to say this to my face?" the old lady sputtered. She had been appalled before, but this was obviously beyond anything she had ever experienced. "Are you lost to all sense of decency?" She wagged a gnarled finger at Phoebe. "I can see now that you are nothing but an impudent strumpet—"

"Aunt Charlotte," Charles interrupted her. "Please remember that you are speaking to the woman who is soon to become my wife."

Aunt Charlotte blanched. "Never tell me that you still intend to wed this—this hussy! After what she has just admitted! For heaven's sake, Charles, think of the family!"

While Aunt Charlotte was speaking, Phoebe, who felt the inexpertly tied pillow beginning to slip, took the opportunity to ease herself into a nearby chair. Burying her face in a handkerchief, she gave all the appearance of weeping softly into it, though in reality she was trying desperately to stifle a growing bubble of laughter. This charade was even more entertaining than she had anticipated.

"Certainly I intend to marry Phoebe," Charles was saying. "And I will not have you or anyone else insulting or upsetting her in any way. As you can see—" He directed a quelling look at his afflicted fiancée. "She is barely able to control her emotions." What on earth, he wondered, had prompted Phoebe to such a mad-brained scheme as this? To behave in this outrageous fashion! Had she no thought for her reputation, or was it that she could not resist any opportunity of vexing him? Everything she did seemed calculated to compromise them both beyond hope of recovery.

"Well," said his aunt, rising from her chair with regal dignity, "I have heard quite enough for one day. And that which I never expected to hear in my lifetime! Especially from you, Charles. If you are so besotted with this female that you can forget all principle and duty, I wash my hands of you. You are a disgrace to the family name.

"As for you, Dorothy," she flung at Mrs. Hargood, the pink and purple feathers in her turban bobbing wildly, "if you can condone this atrocity, you are not the woman I thought I knew. I only hope you may not live to regret your rash actions. But for myself, I do not mean to set foot in this house again as long as I live. I had as soon pay a visit to Sodom and Gomorra!"

She ended this display of high dudgeon by attempting to sweep from the room. Indeed, had not the fringe of her gown caught in the door as she tried to close it, her exit would have been perfect. Even with this disadvantage, she still managed to maintain a certain air of dignity, directing a powerful glare at Charles before she closed the door behind her for a second, and last, time.

"Phoebe, you are a wonder!" Mrs. Hargood cried, much to her son's disgust. "But do you think you ought to have done anything so—so unusual?"

"Unusual?" Charles said. "Unprecedented and unforgivable would be nearer to the mark."

"But it was splendidly done!" his mother contradicted, not noticeably abashed by his disapproval. "I have never seen anything like it, indeed."

Charles disposed himself comfortably on the sofa, eyeing Phoebe critically. "That is only because you missed her most remarkable performance in my bedchamber on Tuesday morning. Believe me, it would be hard to choose which was the most diverting."

Phoebe, emerging from her handkerchief, accepted these plaudits as her due. "It is a gift," she said, with a saucy look at Charles.

"You are certainly gifted at creating havoc," he agreed. "What other accomplishments do you possess, I wonder?"

"That is for you to discover after we are wed!"

"I shudder at the very thought!"

"You have never been able to appreciate Phoebe!" Letty cried, coming to the defence of her friend.

Aside from a faintly raised eyebrow, Charles ignored this remark. "We may all be thankful for Aunt Charlotte's peculiar habits, at least. She is something of a recluse," he added, at Phoebe's inquiring look. "Her visits here are rare enough, and it sometimes goes several years that she does not leave her house. Therefore the tale of this morning's escapade is not likely to go any farther than her few cronies in the village."

"So I gathered," Phoebe said. "I had never even heard of her before today."

"And so," he commented unsmilingly, "you felt you might proceed with impunity."

It was as well that he expected no contrition, for Phoebe displayed none. "Exactly so, Charles," she said, apparently pleased by his discernment. "And it *was* entertaining, was it not?"

"Excessively," he agreed with a wry look.

"I enjoyed it enormously," Mrs. Hargood said. "It is so exactly what that horrid old woman needed. She is dreadfully high in the instep, you know."

"You are the perfect mother-in-law!" cried Phoebe. "So sympathetic and understanding. Charles, I expect, takes after his papa."

"He is the very image of my dear Phillip." Mrs. Hargood gazed fondly upon her son. "I can only pray that you are as happy with Charles as I was with his father."

There was a distinctly watery look to her eyes as she spoke, a look with which Charles was quite familiar. Though it had been some fifteen years since his father's death, his mother had never really gotten over the loss. There were moments when Charles was aware of a certain emptiness in his own life, for he and his father had been very close.

"This is not the time to be maudlin," he said.

"No, indeed," Phoebe concurred, catching the sadness in Mrs. Hargood's eyes and wholly missing the look in the son's. "It is a time to rejoice. We have just rid ourselves of a thoroughly disagreeable old woman."

Charles favored her with a smile of quite genuine gratitude and humor. Slightly shocked, Phoebe realized she had seldom seen such a smile on his lips. She found herself wishing that she might see it more often. He was decidedly attractive when he smiled so.

"Not *we*," Charles corrected her. "All the credit for that singular feat belongs to you, Phoebe. I must say that you have achieved what I had believed impossible. I've known Aunt Charlotte all my life, and today is the very first time that I have ever seen her put out of countenance. My compliments, ma'am."

"Am I forgiven for my outrageous behavior, then?" she asked, her head tilted in inquiry.

"I will gladly forgive you," Charles said, rising, "if you will promise to try and curb your penchant for amateur theatricals."

"I promise you, my dear Charles, that such unbecoming spectacles are a thing of the past."

As Phoebe stood up to emphasize her point, however, the forgotten pillow was loosed from its moorings and slid down the front of her gown to land with a fat "plop" at her feet.

"Oh Charles!" she cried, lifting the downy bundle in her arms. "Our firstborn!"

This was too deliciously absurd. Letty and Mrs. Hargood immediately fell into whoops, while Phoebe much enjoyed the sight of Charles trying unsuccessfully to maintain a straight face. His lips quivered in spite of his best efforts.

Eventually the ladies gained some control over their mirth and wiped their streaming eyes. They were about to return to the sitting room and some unfinished stitching when Charles forestalled them. "I would be grateful, Mama, if you and Miss Comston could spare Phoebe for a few minutes. I have something to discuss with her. You need not worry, I shall not detain her very long."

"You do not mean to lecture or scold her, sir?" Letty was still inclined to be suspicious of her host's motives.

Charles addressed her gravely. "I assure you, I shall not."

"Do not be such a goose, Letty," Phoebe said. "Charles may have many unpleasant qualities, but he is not an ogre."

"Thank you, ma'am," Charles said, appearing much affected. "That is the closest to a compliment I have ever received from you."

As Letty and Mrs. Hargood were about to leave, Simpson appeared at the door.

"Ah! Simpson," Phoebe greeted him gaily, "how opportune! Would you have Gladys return this pillow to my room for me? I cannot think why I should have brought it down!"

"Very good, madam," Simpson replied, his voice perfectly expressionless, but his eyes moving from Phoebe to the pillow and back again. Phoebe could well imagine what he must be thinking of the very odd female who was soon to be mistress here.

He retired without comment, and Mrs. Hargood led the giggling Letitia away in search of needles.

"Now, Charles," Phoebe said, turning to him once more, "I believe you had something you wished to say to me."

There was a moment's pause as Charles tried to collect his thoughts. He was not eager to open this conversation. What they had to discuss was no great matter, but it brought their impending marriage that much closer. It was difficult too, to concentrate on his subject while Phoebe was standing there looking so pretty in her blue frock. Blue was perhaps not really her best color, but a woman of her beauty would be arresting in sackcloth and ashes.

Charles knew a moment of real shame at the realization that he felt not a particle of regret for the departure of Olivia. In all honesty, he was more relieved than anything, for he had been having serious doubts about wedding her. His feelings for her had been tepid at best. Phoebe, however, was another matter. It was impossible to deny that she was beautiful, and he was aware of a certain perverse satisfaction in knowing that he would be envied by many men. But he could never be entirely comfortable in her presence. Whenever she was near, it was as if the very air was charged with an indefinable something which could neither be explained nor ignored.

He only knew that he must be on his guard against her.

Now he feared that it was too late. Life with Phoebe would be anything but placid, as her conduct the previous half hour had clearly shown. Still, he could hardly draw back at this point.

"Well?" Phoebe asked, puzzled by his long silence. "What is it, Charles? If your face grows any longer, I shall have difficulty in distinguishing it from a ladder."

"I think," he said, passing over her comment, "that we had better make preparations for our removal to London."

"Is that all? I quite thought someone must have died! But as to the journey, I leave it all in your most capable hands."

"You will be staying with us, of course."

Phoebe carefully arranged the folds of her skirt as she seated herself. "Do you think that would be wise, considering our peculiar situation? The wedding is but a few weeks away, after all. I could easily put up at Grillons."

"As you wish," he replied with some reluctance. "But I know my mother will not like it. And no more do I."

Toying absently with the pendant of her earring, Phoebe considered this. "I think it will be best for me to stay with Letitia. Her mother is the most biddable creature and will certainly not mind a little extra company."

"She must be biddable indeed to allow you to have charge of her daughter. I wonder what she will think of this affair?"

"Believe me," Phoebe said with a laugh, "the Comston household would make any behavior of mine seem the acme of respectability by comparison. Mr. Comston has a decided preference for ladies of easy virtue. They are his only source of amusement. His wife cares for nothing but her pugs. And Letitia is the most incredible combination of innocence and worldly wisdom that I have ever encountered."

"Well, then, I suppose you will be quite at home there," said her betrothed.

Phoebe gave him a sharp look from under half-closed lids.

"There is no need for sarcasm, dear Charles. The Comstons are very well-connected and are received everywhere—despite their oddities. There will be far less gossip if I stay with them than if I were to remain with you and your mother."

"For once," he assented grudgingly, "you have a sensible idea. We must be as circumspect as possible. I have no doubt that our friends' tongues are already wagging faster than a puppy's tail."

"I wonder what your sister will think of it all?"

Charles scowled at this unnecessary question. "She will not be pleased, of that we can be certain.

Olivia is one of her closest friends."

"I am sure that Hortense will sustain this blow with her usual fortitude."

"You are not very fond of her, are you?" Charles asked, noting the distinctly ironic tone in Phoebe's voice.

Phoebe crossed her arms as if to restrain herself. "Let us simply say that, having met Aunt Charlotte, I can perceive a great resemblance to your sister. Hortense," she added quietly, "is one of the most objectionable women I know. I find it hard to believe that she is actually related to you and your mother."

Charles hardly knew what to reply to this. In truth, he was more than half inclined to agree with Phoebe. Being a man of strong family ties, he truly cared for his sister. But with all the goodwill in the world, he could not bring himself to like her. Since her marriage into the peerage, she had become the most infuriating snob in the kingdom. And worse, she had convinced herself that she was capable of running not only their mother's life, but his as well. What was more, he knew that she was not fond of Phoebe, either. Before, he had always concurred with her opinon on that matter. He hoped she would have the good sense to alter her manner toward Phoebe in future, even if she did not alter her estimation of her.

Picking up a pretty porcelain shepherdess from a nearby table, he turned it over absently in his hands. "I expect you will want to purchase some new clothes while you are in town," he said, changing the subject. "I will supply you with the necessary money—"

Phoebe sprang to her feet. "You will do no such thing!" she cried, Hortense forgotten. "I am perfectly capable of paying for my own clothes."

"Nonsense," Charles said, his face plainly mirroring his annoyance. "There is no need to be so defensive. I was only—"

"You were only being your usual officious self. But I have never allowed you to dictate to me, and I will certainly not do so when we are married."

Charles deposited the pink-and-white shepherdess on the table with a snap, nearly shattering its fragile loveliness.

"I have no intention of dictating to you. But neither will I tolerate your usual high-handed behavior toward me. I will be master in my own home!"

"Are we to argue every time we speak?" Phoebe asked, suddenly aware that she was not enjoying this at all.

"I certainly have no desire to do so. I'm afraid that we are both going to find it difficult to adjust to our—situation."

Seeing that his brief spurt of anger had subsided, Phoebe ventured to inquire, "Shall we still continue with our charade of being in love?"

"I think we should," Charles said after only a moment's hesitation. "As I have said, no one will expect any public demonstration of our affection."

"Such as my performance at breakfast on Tuesday?" she quizzed.

"Precisely."

"As I recall, you handled the situation with considerable skill." At the memory of his "skill," Phoebe felt her heart pounding unaccountably. Quickly she added, "At any rate, you need not fear. I have promised to behave myself, and I always keep my word."

"Then it is settled. Can you be ready by the day after tomorrow?"

"Of course," she answered, moving toward the door.

But she wondered if either of them was really prepared to face a lifetime together. She had hardly dared to dwell on what life would be like as Charles's wife. Strangely, it was not as daunting a prospect as she might once have imagined.

But then, it was one thing to plan a marriage of convenience here in the country, and quite another to find oneself in London on the brink of matrimony. Phoebe had a feeling that things would change greatly when they got to town.

Chapter Four

To London they went. But, as they had feared, their reputation went before them. By the time they reached the city, rumors and speculations of the wildest sort were rampant. Members of the *ton*, who had feared a rather dull season, pounced upon the extraordinary news of their betrothal with all the eagerness of a pack of hounds after an unfortunate fox.

Phoebe and Charles were amazed at the curious twists the story had taken. It was reported that Charles had been caught climbing out of Phoebe's bedroom window; that Phoebe had received a black eye in a brawl with Olivia; that Charles had wept copiously as he begged Olivia to release him; and that Phoebe had deliberately trapped Charles into marriage to get her hands on his considerable fortune.

To be fair, there were a number of people who knew both Charles and Phoebe well enough to dismiss the majority of the gossip which enlivened the sitting rooms and closets of the nation. In fact, two distinct factions developed, each convinced of the justice and accuracy of their positions, and each loudly proclaiming their various opinions.

The first camp felt that Charles and Phoebe were a sly pair who had pulled the wool over everyone's eyes while hiding a scandalous affair. The second party insisted it was no such thing: that this was obviously a marriage of convenience forced upon the unfortunate couple in order to save two reputations tarnished by malicious slander.

As for the engaged pair themselves, it was difficult to decide which group they found most annoying. Their detractors, fueled by the tales of Mrs. Loftbury and her daughter, eyed Charles and Phoebe with morbid curiosity. Their defenders were almost worse, looking upon them as objects of pity and commiseration.

One fact was undeniable, however: neither Mr. Hargood nor his lovely bride-to-be had ever been so popular. Charles, in particular, was exciting an interest which his previous sedate behavior had never before encouraged. They were invited everywhere, and no gathering of distinction could be considered complete without their presence.

Everyone was agog to see them—and especially to see them together, so that they might judge the truth of the matter. Charles, disgusted by the entire affair, reacted typically, becoming more stolid and stiff than ever and giving set-downs to several people foolish enough to allude to the subject in a way he thought offensive. Phoebe, on the other hand, enjoyed the situation hugely. She played one side against the other—now exclaiming rapturously to one friend over her great good fortune, and then bewailing her fate to another.

On public occasions, Phoebe and Charles behaved very much as planned. They were a great deal more cordial toward one another than heretofore, but by no means did they hang upon each other's sleeve or display any great inclination to be always together. But it mattered little how they conducted themselves. If they showed only cool politeness, they were accused by one party or another of trying to hoax everyone with sham respectability. Others, meanwhile, shook their heads sadly at this obvious attempt to make the best of a bad bargain. If they stood up together at a ball, it was remarked on one hand that they danced too well together for them to have ever been real enemies, and on the other, that their acting ability was amazing.

This constant scrutiny and the attendant conjecture at length became too excessive even for Phoebe's sense of humor. She confessed as much to Charles one afternoon as they sat together in Mrs. Comston's drawing room, discussing the final preparations for their wedding.

"Another week of this and I shall go completely distracted! I do not know which I find more irritating in our friends: their suspicion or their solicitude!"

Charles nodded. "I am not overly fond of town life," he admitted. "But I must confess that I have never looked forward to quitting London with quite so much eagerness."

Phoebe looked at him in some consternation. "You do not mean to remove to Camberley before the season ends?"

"Why not?"

"You are such a slow-top, Charles! Only think how dull it will be in the country at this time of year. There is so much more to do here in town."

He scratched his cheek, a puzzled look on his face. "But only a moment ago you said that you were going distracted here."

"How ungallant of you to use my own words against me," she said, pouting. "In any case, I am sure the gossip will die down after our marriage. Then we may both be comfortable again."

"If you prefer town life to the country, I am surprised that you sold Robert's London house," Charles said, eyeing her rather curiously.

Phoebe paused and looked down at the hands folded in her lap. She was a little hesitant about revealing too much to this man. But after all, Charles could certainly be trusted to hold his tongue. Good heavens! He was soon to be her husband, so what reason could there possibly be for withholding such information? In any case,

Charles had doubtless known his cousin well enough to comprehend how he was likely to have conducted his finances, and with what results.

"There were—certain debts—which had to be discharged," she acknowledged. "And I could hardly sell Chesworth Hall. It has been in Robert's family since before Cromwell!"

"Chesworth Hall is a lovely old place," Charles said. "But you will now have a new home. Camberley is not half so grand, but I hope that you will be happy there."

Phoebe caught the rather diffident note in his voice. No man liked to think that he was offering a woman less than she already possessed. Knowing that nothing could be more galling to a man's pride, Phoebe hastened to reassure Charles.

"Camberley is a delightful house," she said sincerely. "Much more comfortable than Chesworth, really. I have always loved to come and stay there with your mother." She did not think it necessary to add that she had generally chosen her visits to coincide with his absences. The gleam in his eye led her to believe that he suspected as much anyway.

Unexpectedly, he reached across to take her hand in his. "Thank you, my dear. I am glad that you like our home. Of course, you shall have a free hand in making any changes you may desire. Your taste, as I know, is always impeccable."

Phoebe, thrown off balance by both the compliment and the warmth of his clasp, could only stammer, "I—I am not likely to change much at Camberley, Charles. But I would be grateful if you would take Chesworth in charge. No one can doubt your talent in managing an estate."

"Naturally, I will do all that I can for you, Phoebe."

"It is no bad thing for a woman to have property of her own. I do not come to you destitute,

Charles."

"Of course not," he said, his eyes warm and his hold on her hand tightening. "Never think that I would ask you to part with your own house. After all, it will be a fine inheritance one day for your children."

In an instant, the atmosphere between them changed. For the first time Phoebe realized that her children would be his children, too. In a week—no, less!—they would be husband and wife. They had never discussed the subject, of course, but she had always wanted a family. And every man must want a son to carry on his name—even Charles. But the thought of bearing Charles a son and all that such a thing entailed was both new and unsettling—especially with her hand held so firmly in his.

His gaze was so earnest and steadfast, his face quite close to hers. Was he going to kiss her again? What an absurd fancy! But the room seemed to have grown very small. A strange but not unpleasant feeling of intimacy grew between them, and Phoebe wondered if Charles had been struck by the same realization as she. Not since that morning in Charles's bedchamber had she been so confused. But then, she had never been this close to him since that fateful day. The uncomfortable silence continued to lengthen, as Charles seemed as tongue-tied as she.

Before either of them could venture to speak, however, they were forestalled by the arrival of Letty. She had come, she said in her usual exuberant manner, to go shopping with Phoebe.

In spite of her continued disapproval of the match, Letty would hardly have been a woman had she not enjoyed helping Phoebe choose her bride clothes and the innumerable accessories required by a lady of fashion.

"Oh," Phoebe said in some confusion, disengaging her hand from Charles's. "I had quite forgotten our little excursion. Pray excuse me, Charles, but I did promise Letty."

Phoebe allowed herself to be led away by Letitia, and perhaps she only imagined the look of relief on Charles's face as he bid her good-bye. She determined to think no more about him as they made their way to the Burlington Arcade for a few hours spent searching for interesting items. This fascinating emporium contained enough gewgaws to keep Phoebe amused for some time. There were fans and reticules, snuff boxes and silk stockings, rouge and ribbons—everything, as her old aunt used to say, except salvation.

Letty chattered away happily, though Phoebe was far too preoccupied to comprehend more than half of what she said. But if Letty noticed her companion's behavior, she made no protest and seemed content to talk on without any response.

Phoebe thought of her life at Chesworth Hall since Robert's death. How large and lonely the place was. It had never felt like home, even when Robert was alive. Now it was a place she was glad to quit for her smaller, more intimate rented house whenever she came to town. Camberley was much more to her taste. The ridiculous thing was that Camberley and Charles had always been linked together in her mind. Even when Charles was not there, she had felt his presence everywhere about the place. How odd that she had never realized it before.

Lost in her musings, Phoebe was suddenly distracted from her pleasant purpose in a most unpleasant manner. They had left the bazaar to find the shop of a modiste who was now all the crack and who had just completed the loveliest gown for Phoebe to wear that night at Almack's. Scarcely had they arrived at Madame Vidal's, however, when they were approached by a stunning redhead, who was evidently also a patron of the establishment. A tall woman, very shapely, she was definitely on the wrong side of thirty.

"Phoebe!" said the stranger, looking the younger woman up and down. "I did not expect to see you here. Ah well, from the looks of it, you are in need of a new gown."

Phoebe tensed instinctively, and even Letty might be forgiven for thinking that she was about to give the woman the cut direct. She did not go so far, but her voice was distinctly curt as she responded. "Good afternoon, Clarissa."

"How pale and drawn you are looking. I vow I scarcely recognized you at first!"

"How odd," Phoebe said. "I was feeling quite well until only a moment ago." Phoebe was aware that Letty was looking at her very curiously, but she did not bother to introduce her friend to the newcomer. It was doubtful that Clarissa would be interested in making Letty's acquaintance in any case; such friends as Clarissa possessed were rarely female.

"My dear," Clarissa's voice penetrated the roaring in Phoebe's ears. "I have only just returned to town myself and have heard the most amazingly silly story. Apparently, it is the latest *on-dit*—but so deliciously absurd! That rattle, Freddy Westcote, acquainted me with it last night, and I vow I could not keep from laughing for a thousand pounds.

"It seems that the whole of London is convinced that you are going to marry Charles Hargood!" With the merest pause for breath, Clarissa continued, "Of course I told Freddy that such a tale could not possibly be true. Even you could not be such a simpleton as to ally yourself with that blockhead."

Phoebe said a silent prayer that she might be able to control herself. Though she would never admit as much, Clarissa Stainford's grandfather had been a mere mill owner in the wilds of Yorkshire. But his granddaughter had beauty and cunning enough to marry above her station: an elderly baronet who died most conveniently in the third year of their marriage, leaving his widow to enjoy a life of wealth and ease. While her morals might make any Cyprian blush, lady Stainford's fashion sense and the lineage of her late husband had cemented her position in polite society.

Clarissa was obviously well aware that Phoebe's engagement to Charles was genuine, and the whole of her artless recital was designed as a lesson in humiliation. Her adversary was a formidable one, as Phoebe knew too well, but this was no time for retreat. Never let it be said that Phoebe Bridgerton was faint-hearted. She might not win the encounter, but she would go down fighting.

"I am afraid," Phoebe said sweetly, "that you owe Mr. Westcote an apology, Clarissa. You are mistaken on all counts. I am no simpleton. Charles is no blockhead. And I most certainly am going to marry him." There. Let her top that.

Clarissa's feigned look of surprise was a masterpiece of mimicry. "Oh!" she cried. "Pray forgive me, Phoebe. I had no idea that things had come to such a desperate pass with you. To be forced to make do with Charles Hargood after a man like Robert!"

Phoebe flicked a speck of dust from her sleeve. "You waste your sympathy, Clarissa. I am perfectly content with my lot."

"How brave you are," Clarissa said with a wide-eyed look. "But there is no need to pretend with me, you know. I was far too well acquainted with Robert to believe that any woman would prefer his cousin. Charles may be a very worthy man, but I doubt that a life of dull respectability will be a satisfying substitute for what you once had."

Phoebe was growing heartily sick of Charles being always compared so unfavorably with his cousin. True, he had not Robert's boyish charm or classical good looks, but in his own way he was quite an attractive man—well-favored and well-built, even though of no more than average height. He was worth ten feckless husbands like Robert. In fact, it was high time someone spoke up on behalf of this much maligned gentleman. And who better than herself?

"I am sure that no one knew my late husband better than you," Phoebe answered her tormentor. "But I think you do not know Charles Hargood at all. I, on the other hand, am intimately acquainted with him and can assure you that he possesses—abilities—which even Robert might have envied. There are few people who know Charles really well. But I," she added with a smile of calculated mystery, "have been privileged to see a side of him the world knows nothing of. Believe me, Clarissa, I consider myself the most fortunate of women!"

This panegyric for her betrothed succeeded too well in its object. Clarissa might not be sure just how sincere it was, but Phoebe could tell that her interest was well and truly piqued. Later, Phoebe would have time to regret arousing this woman's apparent interest in Charles, but for now she felt the flush of victory.

"Then it seems," Clarissa said at last, "that I must congratulate you on having made a fine catch. I hope you will be as happy in your second marriage as in your first."

Phoebe's smile grew. "I look forward to being even happier."

"I suppose you and Charles will be at the Pendletons' ball tonight?" Clarissa said, unaccountably changing the subject.

"I have promised to chaperon my young friend

here to Almack's," Phoebe answered, belatedly remembering Letty's existence.

"And is Charles to accompany you?"

"He is to attend a card party at Mrs. Burchell's."

For some reason, Clarissa seemed inordinately pleased at this information. "We have had such a pleasant chat, I vow! What a happy chance for us to meet like this. It has been…most illuminating!" In a moment she had whirled away, leaving the air in the small shop heavy with her expensive scent—the gift, no doubt, of one of her numerous admirers.

Letty craned her neck to catch a last glimpse. "How rude! But she is very smart looking. Is she really a friend of yours?"

Phoebe could not help laughing at Letty's incredulous tone. "That depends on one's point of view," she said. "Clarissa was once Robert's mistress."

~/~

Not until Phoebe had received her gown from the hands of Madame Vidal herself and they returned to their carriage, did Letty venture to speak. "Phoebe, what did you mean?"

Phoebe, settling herself into her seat, affected bewilderment. "About what?" she asked.

"About Lady Stainford, of course!" Letty cried, not at all deceived.

Clutching her packages, Phoebe hesitated a moment. "I think you had best forget my rash words, Letty. I should never have spoken at all. You are much too young to be burdened with such knowledge."

"Do you mean that she and Robert were…friends before your marriage?" Letty insisted. "Surely it could not have been after—"

Phoebe pinched her arm mercilessly. "I wish

you would learn to hold your tongue!" she whispered. "Our driver is not deaf, you know. If you will have the truth, you must be content to wait until we are alone in the house."

Letty was forced to restrain herself, and the remainder of the drive was conducted in complete and very uncomfortable silence. Each had to be content with her own thoughts until they drew up before the front door of the Comston home. They alighted as sedately as possible and made their way inside and up to Phoebe's room. Letty was obviously famished with curiosity, but Phoebe was not eager to satisfy it. Even after all this time, the subject was still painful.

"Well?" Letty asked, sitting on the edge of Phoebe's bed and looking up at her like a child eager to be told a story at bedtime. Perhaps now was as good a time as any for her to learn that life is no fairy tale and that happy endings are rare indeed.

"My husband," Phoebe said slowly, "was involved with Lady Stainford for almost a year before his death."

Letty's eyes opened wide as she tried to comprehend this incredible pronouncement. "Oh Phoebe! No!"

"Oh Letty—yes!" her friend contradicted. "And I am fairly certain that Clarissa was not the first or only one."

"But—but your marriage was a love match! Everyone said you were perfect for each other. You were so happy together."

Phoebe hated to see her friend so distressed as youthful illusions began to crumble like stale wedding cake. Sighing softly, Phoebe did not falter in her tale: "For the first year we were happy—very much so. But by then I had already begun to realize that I had made a terrible mistake in marrying Robert. I had fallen in love with a man who existed only in my imagination."

"What do you mean?"

Phoebe settled down beside her friend and cast her thoughts back seven years. "When I first met Robert," she began, "he seemed to me the very image of every romantic hero I had ever read about. He was tall, handsome, bold, and reckless. I was very young and naive, I'm afraid, and took him—quite literally—at face value. He was my knight in shining armor.

"But after we married, I discovered that beneath the armor was not the strong and noble hero of my dreams. Instead, I found a wild, spoilt and impetuous child who refused to grow up. He seemed to have no notion that marriage should make any difference to his way of life."

Letty squeezed her hand sympathetically. "He did not love you?"

"I believe he thought he did," Phoebe said, attempting to be fair to the memory of the dead. "Perhaps he had as much love for me as it was possible for him to give to anyone."

"But he was unfaithful to you!"

Phoebe shrugged. "He was very susceptible to beautiful women, and with his looks it was fatally easy for him to have almost any woman who took his fancy. Then, too, he had grown up in a very different set from my own, where such things as marital fidelity were not considered of much importance, and his wealth and position only increased his tendency to self-indulgence."

"I never imagined such a thing," Letty whispered.

"How should you?" Phoebe patted her young friend's hand before resuming her recital. "Everything was a game to Robert, you see. He played at love just as he played at life.

"At first, I tried to match him. I learned to drive to an inch, and even had a high-perch phaeton built expressly for the purpose. I played all games of chance and danced until my legs felt like two frayed ribbons. But it was useless. I was wearing myself out, and my husband was going his own way. Perhaps if we had had a child, it might have been different. Who can say?"

Phoebe knew in her heart that it was unlikely. Robert was as unsuited to be a father as he was to be a husband. Like most women, she had eventually accepted her situation. She lived her life and he lived his. By the time she learned of his infidelity, she no longer cared enough to be greatly distressed by it. Her worst fear was that his addiction to gaming would put them both in the Fleet.

What hurt the most in the end was that she became an object of pity. Everyone knew or suspected what was happening. One of her friends—a patroness of Almack's, no less—actually had the audacity to suggest that she find herself a lover. As long as she was discreet, of course—like her husband!

Phoebe had indeed flirted with several gentlemen who would not have objected to a closer connection. But she had been raised in the country, where such things were not easily accepted. Her vows still meant something to her, if they did not to Robert. No one was ever able to accuse her of breaking them. In her eyes, that would have made her no better than Clarissa.

Letty was almost in tears by now. "Yet you never betrayed him?" she asked. "Even though he betrayed you?"

"Let us simply say that I always play by the rules, whether at cards or at love," Phoebe replied. "But the truth is that when Robert died, although I was sad for what might have been, my greatest feeling was one of intense relief. Do you know how he died, by the way?"

"Was it not of a fever?"

"Yes. But do you know how he contracted that fever?" A wry smile pulled up the corners of Phoebe's lips. "One of his friends wagered that he would not ride naked on horseback through the streets of Coventry—a sort of latter-day male Godiva!"

"Who?" Letty asked, mystified.

"Never mind," her friend said with a chuckle. "Suffice it to say that Robert never turned down a wager, however absurd. He made his famous ride—after midnight, I am happy to say, when few of the citizens were awake to observe the spectacle."

"And that's when he caught a chill…"

Phoebe nodded. "Had he possessed the good sense to wait until July or August, all might have been well," she said. "But, impatient as ever, he set out immediately. He won his bet on the third day of January and lost his life several days later. He died quite as foolishly as he had lived."

"Oh Phoebe," Letty cried. "How horrible it all is!"

"I should have listened to my mother," Phoebe admitted ruefully. "She never did approve of the marriage, though when I insisted upon it she was too weak willed to forbid it. I am glad now that she did not live long enough to see her fears for me come true."

"Are all men like Robert, do you think?" Letty asked, looking most perturbed.

"Of course not. I cannot imagine Charles behaving in such a fashion, can you?"

"No, indeed!" Letty agreed emphatically. "And I am sure my dearest Henry would not, either."

As Phoebe knew only too well, Henry was Letitia's childhood sweetheart. Phoebe had so often listened to the younger girl's rapturous recital of his manifold virtues, that the very mention of his name made her ill. Henry sounded terribly dull to her, but Letty worshipped him with childish obstinacy, in spite of the fact that he had shown not the slightest interest in her for the past two years or more. "I am sure that Henry would never do such a thing," Phoebe said at her driest.

Letitia, meanwhile, seemed to have been struck by a novel idea. "Perhaps Charles is the husband for you after all!"

Phoebe's brows drew together. "To be honest," she said, "I never had any intention of marrying again. Once was more than enough. My only real pleasure in the last few years has been the enjoyment I receive from baiting Charles. And it seems I must now forego even that."

"When you spoke to Lady Stainford today," Letty said, laughing, "you almost had me convinced that you and Charles were lovers."

"Poor Charles. He certainly did not deserve that woman's condescension. Well, I have given her food for thought."

Standing up and smoothing the ruffled counterpane, Letty commented, "She must believe Charles to be something quite out of the common way now."

Phoebe did not find this particularly amusing. Instead, she felt most uncomfortable at the idea that Clarissa might be intrigued by her former lover's despised cousin. "We have quite lost track of the time," she said hurriedly. "We had best go and make ourselves ready, if we are not to be late."

Letty was already halfway to the door. "Yes, I'm going," she said. "But I'm glad we had this talk, Phoebe. And I hope that horrid Lady Stainford gets just what she deserves someday."

Phoebe gave an exasperated sigh. "It will be best if you forget Clarissa altogether, and do not dwell on what I told you today. Now make haste. We are wasting time!"

Letty obediently left the room after giving her

friend an exaggerated hug and a kiss on the cheek. But in spite of her own admonition to hurry, Phoebe sat quite still for a long time after Letty's departure, frowning at the face reflected in her dressing table mirror. Clarissa and Charles…

No, no! It was impossible. And yet…

"If he should ever kiss Clarissa—" she thought idiotically. If that were to happen, Phoebe hardly dared conjecture what the outcome might be!

Chapter Five

Almack's Assembly Rooms might well be considered one of the dullest and most unimpressive establishments in England.

But, as Phoebe was aware, admittance into the hallowed halls insured social acceptance, and the holder of one of the cherished vouchers was fortunate indeed. To this celebrated address on King Street, the members of the *beau monde* flocked in the hope of making useful connections by which they might barter a promising son or daughter for a title, a fortune—or both, if it was at all possible. Phoebe had long ago lost her enthusiasm for this palace of pomposity, but to Letty it was all new—a place of endless fascination and expectation. As they made their entrance together, more than one head was turned and more than one quizzing glass raised to survey so exquisite a pair.

Letitia was radiant in a demure white gown embroidered with pale-blue forget-me-nots to match her sparkling eyes and the silken flowers in her golden hair.

As an experienced young widow who had long since cut her eye-teeth, Phoebe no longer affected such maidenly styles. She wore one of Madame Vidal's most enticing creations: a low-cut gown of bottle-green taffeta with gold silk trim. Her luxuriant dark hair, simply dressed and curled, was held by a small jeweled comb, and her fan resembled a gilded peacock.

The rooms were already full when they arrived, and Phoebe felt that she could hardly blame Charles for absenting himself from this place. Had it not been for her promise to help launch Letty into polite society, she would probably have done the same. She settled herself upon a strategically placed chair and prepared for an evening of unalleviated boredom.

"Do you see anybody?" Letty asked presently, in an awed whisper.

Since they were surrounded by a crowd of people who resembled nothing so much as a brood of over-dressed chickens clucking and scratching in a barnyard, Phoebe was a little perplexed at this question. "I am certainly not blind," she said. "I can see that there are a good many anybodies here."

"No, no!" Letty cried impatiently. "Do you see anyone you know—anybody important?"

Phoebe glanced around the room with slow deliberation. "I see a number of old acquaintances. But, as Charles once remarked, one is not likely to find anyone of the least importance at Almack's."

"And as I often heard you remark, Charles is a prating fool!"

Phoebe was genuinely surprised. "Did I say that? I suppose I must have thought it witty at the time. But it was also unjust."

Letty giggled childishly. "You seem as determined now to defend Charles as you once were to insult him."

"Well, I cannot be forever laughing at my own husband, can I? Though I know some women who do."

"Oh, never mind Charles," Letty said, tired of this conversation. "Is that not Lady Jersey?"

For the next three quarters of an hour, Phoebe was occupied in pointing out notable personages and introducing Letitia to those who were of least danger to a green girl.

Letty was most impressed by the top-lofty patronesses of Almack's and wondered aloud to

Phoebe whether they had had many lovers in their time. Phoebe once more minded Letty to hold her tongue, lest she commit some dreadful *faux pas* which would forever bar her from society.

But Phoebe need not have worried. Letty was a pretty and lively girl, who was soon surrounded by admiring gentlemen. She was invited to join the next set, and Phoebe watched her dance a quadrille with considerable verve. After that, Letty never wanted for a partner, and Phoebe resigned herself to the tedium involved in playing the staid chaperone.

"How very serious you look, my dear Mrs. Bridgerton," a masculine voice sounded at her elbow. "I detect the fell hand of Charles Hargood."

Phoebe turned to stare up at the gentleman beside her.

He was a tall man, over six feet, with strikingly blond good looks which always reminded her of Robert. In fact, he had been one of her husband's best friends. "Douglas!" she cried. "You rogue! It is months since I last saw you, and you greet me in such a fashion. You deserve a proper set-down."

Smiling, he raised her hand to his lips. "I shall not cry pardon. You are the cruelest woman alive," he continued with a comically wounded look. "When I think of the times you have spurned my offers of marriage! And now to find that I have been passed over in favor of Charles Hargood. It is insupportable!"

"Oh." Phoebe was enjoying this old game between them. Their flirtation had always been the most fun, since each was well aware that the other was not in the least bit serious. "Shall you call Charles out?"

"Were Charles not such a fine shot, I might even do that."

Phoebe was frankly astonished. "Is he so?"

"One of the best," Douglas acknowledged. "Dueling, however, is not his forte. A fat pigeon or a woodcock may fear his prowess, but I think I may be easy on the head of dueling!"

"What a pity," Phoebe said, with what she hoped was a wistful look. "I have never had two men fight over me, you know. I think I should quite enjoy it, but I fear Charles is not likely to oblige."

Douglas's countenance grew more serious. "Charles is a good man," he conceded. "But when I recall the opinion of him which you have often expressed, it is hard for me to believe that he would be your choice for a husband. And, to be honest, I never heard him say any good of you either."

Phoebe simulated an attitude of amazement. "But Douglas, have you not heard of our absolutely scandalous romance?"

"Indeed, I have heard of little else since I came to town," he said, patently unconvinced. "Had I not been so well acquainted with you, I might even have believed some of these Banbury tales."

"You are not convinced of our attachment, then?"

"Knowing you, I am inclined to be skeptical. You are not the kind to be involved in a clandestine affair."

"Perhaps you do not know me as well as you think," she teased. But for once Douglas was not listening. His gaze was firmly fixed on the couples swirling about the floor—on one couple in particular.

"Phoebe," he said at length. "Do you know the girl in the blue and white gown? I have not seen her before."

"That," she replied, having ascertained the object of his interest, "is Miss Letitia Comston."

He was not satisfied with a mere name, however. "But who is she?" he insisted. "Do you know her people? And, most important, can you procure me an introduction?"

Phoebe was quite amused. This evening was not the dreadful bore she had anticipated. Douglas was obviously more than ordinarily interested in her young friend. It was most unlike him, but perhaps he was getting soft in his old age.

It would probably come to nothing, of course, but if he should form a serious attachment, it would be beyond anything great. Lord Douglas Ardshire was a marquis with far too great a share of wealth and good looks to remain single. It was quite unnatural, Phoebe decided. A much-sought-after *parti*, he would be a marvelous match for Letty. In Phoebe's opinion, Douglas was just the kind of man her friend needed.

"Well?" Douglas was growing impatient at the prolonged silence.

"What a fickle beau you are!" Phoebe chided. "No sooner do we begin a promising flirtation than you promptly desert me in favor of my *protégée*."

He caught eagerly at the last word. "Are you Miss Comston's chaperone then? No wonder I find you sitting here with all the old tabbies! But what good fortune! You can introduce me to my angel yourself."

"Good fortune, indeed," Phoebe agreed. "At the mere thought, your face lights up like one of London's new-fangled gas lamps."

"I suppose," he murmured, "that all her dances are already taken."

Phoebe shook her head sadly. "I fear so," she said. "However, if you are a very good boy, you may have the honor of procuring for us a little supper. But you must behave yourself, mind!"

"I shall be a pattern-card of virtue and civility."

He was as good as his word. When Phoebe

presented him to her charge, he behaved just as he ought, though there was a look in his eyes which none but the innocent Letitia could mistake. Letty, for her part, seemed very pleased with her new acquaintance. Later she confessed to Phoebe that she thought him monstrously handsome and asked Phoebe whether she would not prefer to wed Douglas rather than Charles.

As usual, supper was perfectly awful. But Letty, already warned of Almack's culinary deficiencies, did not seem to mind. She ate heartily, admitting with charming candor that she was absolutely starved. With each minute that passed in her company, Douglas seemed more and more captivated. Upon learning that Phoebe was actually living in the same house as this divine creature, he asked at once when he might be allowed to call on them.

"I am afraid," Phoebe told him bluntly, "that we shall be much too busy in the next few days to receive callers. My wedding is only five days off, you know."

At this information, Douglas looked so woefully downcast that Phoebe relented and offered him some hope. She said that even after her marriage she would still be in town and very much involved in her young friend's presentation to society. If Douglas would only be a little patient, she would insure that he had ample opportunity of meeting the young lady.

"But you must not be trifling with Letty's affections," she warned him. "She is not at all up to snuff, you know, and might easily mistake a flirtation for something more serious."

He was rather offended at that. "Surely you know me better than that, Phoebe!"

"Forgive me," she said, relaxing somewhat. "Letty is my responsibility, but perhaps I am taking it a little too seriously. Anyway," she added with a quizzing look, "I think you would have a difficult time engaging her affections."

"Again you seek to provoke me," he said, grinning. "Call me a coxcomb if you will, but I believe I am generally held to have considerable address and am not incapable of exciting the tender passion in the female breast."

She gave him a sharp rap across the knuckles with her fan. "You are certainly accomplished in the art of flirtation. What you do not realize is that Miss Comston's affections are already engaged."

This was plainly not to his liking, but he insisted on knowing more. So Phoebe kindly explained about Letitia's childhood friend, who was even now in town and to whom Letty considered herself inextricably bound.

"What nonsense." Douglas was inclined to be contemptuous.

"Ordinarily, I would agree with you," Phoebe said, carefully adjusting the sleeve of her gown. "But you have no notion how romantic the poor child is. Her ideas have all been gleaned from sentimental romances, and she sees herself as the faithful lover of her adored Henry—whom, by the bye, she has not seen these three years or more."

His lips compressed tightly, Douglas heard her out before undertaking to reply. "Is there some agreement between them then? Has their marriage been arranged, perhaps?"

"Only in Letty's too-fertile imagination, I fear," Phoebe answered. "I am convinced that the young man is quite unaware of her feelings and may, indeed, have forgotten her existence."

Douglas, his eyes following Letty's progress in the dance, would not have that. "Impossible!" he declared. "One does not forget someone like Miss Comston so easily."

Poor Douglas! He was, indeed, smitten. Phoebe was sure she would derive a great deal of amusement from watching him make sheep's eyes at Letty. At the same time, she had a strong presentiment that his courtship would not be a smooth one. She was just about to warn him of this when she was hailed by no less a person than Lady Sefton.

Maria Sefton was as amiable as she was elegant, and Phoebe always enjoyed her company. After a few moments of inconsequential chit-chat, however, Douglas politely excused himself and soon quit the room altogether.

"My dear Phoebe," said Maria. "It is an age since we have seen you. What good fortune brings you here tonight?"

"I am escorting Miss Letitia Comston."

Maria nodded. "She is quite charming. But you are much too young to be acting the part of staid companion, my dear."

"I thought I might find it amusing," Phoebe admitted.

"And is it?"

"Letty can be quite entertaining in her innocent way."

"Douglas seems to be quite taken with her," Maria said, watching the gentleman's retreating form. "Do I detect a budding romance?"

Phoebe looked once again at Letty, busily charming yet another susceptible young man. "I would not refine too much upon it. The season is young, and Letty has many admirers."

"Well, she is a nice, unassuming sort of girl. She could not do better than Douglas."

Phoebe could not help laughing. "I never knew you to be such a matchmaker, Maria. You have them at the altar already."

"Oh, it is quite settled in my mind," Maria said, not a whit put out by Phoebe's accusation. "They will deal delightfully, mark my words. But what of you, Phoebe?" she asked, regarding her friend with a look of gentle censure. "I have it on the best authority that a certain Duke was eager to make you his Duchess. And what must you do but settle for a plain Mister Hargood!"

"Alas!" Phoebe said, her hand over her heart. "I fear that I suffer from a distressing lack of ambition."

Ignoring this melodramatic outburst, Maria flashed her a mischievous smile. "I do not blame you at all," she said. "In fact, I think you have been much more wise in choosing your second husband than you were with your first." Giving Phoebe no chance to respond, she went on, "But you should not neglect your friends so shamefully, my dear. It has been some time since you last graced us with your presence."

Phoebe gave her a straight look. "To be honest, Maria, I dreaded bringing Letty here tonight. After Robert's death, I avoided Almack's as much as possible. I was always afraid that I might meet Clarissa here. I know it is cowardly," she admitted, "but I felt I could not face her without disgracing myself."

Maria lowered her voice significantly. "If Clarissa is not careful," she said, with a certain degree of satisfaction, "she will be the one who disgraces herself! She takes few pains to hide her latest liaison. Sailing much too close to the wind, if you ask me. But she does not often come here, for which I am thankful."

Phoebe, equally thankful, squeezed Maria's hand in sympathetic understanding. "It is all academic now, at any rate. The meeting I have been avoiding took place this afternoon in a shop. Now that it is past, I feel I can face her without trepidation."

"I am glad," Lady Sefton said. "As a matter of fact, I saw her myself this evening. She informed me that she was going to some card party or other. I was very much surprised. That is not at all

Clarissa's usual style."

A sudden and terrible suspicion seized hold of Phoebe. "Card party?" she said sharply. "Not Mrs. Burchell's card party?"

Maria appeared startled by such uncanny perspicacity. "Now that you mention it, I believe it was Mrs. Burchell's," she said, eyeing Phoebe with considerable respect. "Were you invited as well? I must say it seems an odd place to find Clarissa Stainford. I can only assume that there is some man present in whom she is interested."

Yes indeed, Phoebe thought. There was a man there. She could even have told Maria his name: Charles Hargood. Clarissa was attending that party for one reason only: to seduce Charles. And if Clarissa succeeded, Phoebe had no one but herself to blame.

Oh, why had she painted such a glowing picture to that harpy this afternoon—presenting Charles as an adoring lover? That was all Clarissa needed to spark her interest in a man she had scarcely noticed before. And Charles, for all his strict principles and high-minded morality, was a man like other men. Remembering yet again the warmth of his kiss, Phoebe was very much afraid that he would be all too susceptible to the blandishments of a beautiful woman like Clarissa.

Phoebe did not love Charles herself, of course—the very idea was absurd! But when she considered that she might lose not one but two husbands to that scheming hussy, her stomach revolted. Charles might not be able to wound her heart, but her pride was another matter. Indeed, Robert's betrayal had not hurt half as much as did this prospect of Charles's possible weakness. It must be that the second time was harder to accept than the first.

Whatever the cause, Phoebe was more distressed than she had ever been in her life. Her pleasure in the evening faded and she heard not another word poor Maria addressed to her, though she somehow managed to appear perfectly conscious.

Her mind constantly brought before her the most vivid images of Charles's seduction. By the time Lady Sefton noticed the paleness of her cheeks, Phoebe was able to declare quite truthfully that she had developed a severe headache. She could stay no longer, and quickly sought out Letty to escort that disappointed damsel home.

~ / ~

Had Phoebe been able to witness Lady Stainford's conduct that evening, it would have done her headache no good at all. Rather, it would have increased her affliction, for she had not been unjust in her judgment of Clarissa's motives and morals.

Charles had attended Mrs. Burchell's card party mainly to please his mother, who happened to be one of the hostess's oldest and dearest friends. Like Phoebe, Charles expected a rather dull evening. In fact, he had already made arrangements to leave early for his club and send the carriage back for Mrs. Hargood later. Mrs. Burchell's card parties were safe but unexciting affairs—a mixture of low stakes and high gossip—which did not appeal to most gentlemen under sixtyBut no sooner had he and his mother arrived than he was accosted by a familiar-looking redhead in a revealing gown more suited to a ballroom floor than a humble whist table.

"Charles Hargood! I vow it is ages since I last saw you!" Clarissa cried, grabbing hold of his arm with a proprietary gesture.

Charles was honestly surprised. His acquaintance with the notorious widow was of the slightest, and he was at a loss to understand the meaning

est, and he was at a loss to understand the meaning of this effusive greeting. Moreover, he was acutely aware of his mother looking on with curiosity and disapproval. He was therefore a little diffident in his response. "It is a pleasure to see you again, Lady Stainford."

Clarissa pouted prettily. "How horrid of you to be so formal, Charles," she said. "Surely you know me well enough to call me Clarissa."

Charles hardly knew what to reply. Though not well versed in the art of dalliance, he was neither so green that he could not recognize the tone of Clarissa's voice nor the invitation in her sparkling blue eyes.

She gave him no time to frame an answer, however. "You must do penance for treating me so shabbily, sir!" she declared. "I insist that you be my partner. It must be fate, indeed. You cannot deny me, Charles. We were made to be partners, I vow. Do you not think so, my dear Mrs. Hargood?"

Mrs. Hargood accorded this no more than a most impolite sniff, which Clarissa completely disregarded. So it was that Charles, who had previously promised to partner his mama, found himself sitting at the card table, facing one of the loveliest women in London.

But Clarissa's optimism proved disastrously unfounded.

They most certainly did not play well together. Clarissa was too intent on smiling and flirting with Charles to pay much attention to her cards. And Charles, basking in the novel sensation of being singled out by one of society's acknowledged beauties, found himself too preoccupied with Clarissa to concentrate on his game. Indeed, had the stakes been higher, they might well have lost a fortune between them.

Clarissa seemed perfectly happy, however, and

Charles did not mind his losses until someone asked the time and he realized that he should have left for his club twenty minutes earlier. And to think he had not wanted to come here tonight!

He rose reluctantly to take his leave, apologizing for his abrupt departure. No sooner were the words out of his mouth than Clarissa rose also.

"I wonder if you would be so kind as to give me a ride home in your carriage, Charles?" she asked. "I am not feeling at all the thing, and really fear that to stay any longer would be too much for my constitution."

Since she was looking the picture of good health, Charles was puzzled by this pronouncement. However, he could hardly refuse to assist a lady in distress. Naturally, he assented to her request, and only when she flashed him a knowing smile did he comprehend her curious behavior. It was all a ruse. She wanted to be alone with him in his carriage.

Charles was perplexed. It was one thing to conduct a mild flirtation with a woman across a card table in a crowded room, quite another to be alone with her in a closed conveyance. Especially a woman with the reputation of Lady Stainford. Surely there were enough complications in his life at present without that. But it was his own fault for behaving in so uncharacteristic a manner. It was not even as if he were really attracted to the woman. He did not particularly admire redheads. He preferred dark hair, hazel eyes, a more petite figure, and—his thoughts stopped abruptly, for he realized that the image conjured up of his ideal woman bore a striking resemblance to Phoebe Bridgerton.

For a short time that evening, he had forgotten Phoebe, putting all thought of his impending marriage from his mind. Clarissa's flattering attentions were a balm to his masculine vanity, and a refreshing change from the treatment he usually received at Phoebe's hands. Phoebe had certainly never looked at him with such open invitation, with something even akin to admiration in her eyes. But why should she? Charles Hargood meant nothing to her.

While Clarissa was making her excuses to "her dear Elizabeth," the nondescript woman with whom she had come to the party, Charles went to inform his mother that he was about to leave.

When she understood that Clarissa was to accompany her son, Mrs. Hargood looked at him as if he had just confessed to murder. "Do you think you should go alone with Lady Stainford?" she asked.

Charles's lips compressed. "I am four-and-thirty years old, Mama!" he snapped, annoyed by her patent anxiety. "I believe I may be trusted to refrain from ravishing the woman!"

His mother was obviously shocked at such unprecedented behavior. "Charles!" she cried, staring. "For heaven's sake! Someone may hear you—" But he had already turned and stalked off.

Still fuming over the way his mother and Phoebe acted—as if he knew nothing about the fair sex—Charles escorted Clarissa to the waiting carriage in a dangerously reckless mood. It was a long time since he had been with a woman. He wondered just how far Clarissa intended to carry this game of hers? Well, he was no Don Juan, but he might as well indulge the wench.

He handed her in, placed a rug over her knees to protect her from the chill March air, then got in himself and sat down very deliberately beside her. As they drove off into the darkness, she leaned into the curve of his arm, and the cloyingly sweet scent of her French perfume assailed his nostrils.

"I have been waiting all evening for the chance to be alone with you, Charles," Clarissa said, her hand moving slowly along his thigh. "I never realized before just how attractive you are."

alized before just how attractive you are."

She was certainly a bold piece! Charles doubted if any light-skirt could have come more quickly to the point. Why then did he hesitate? Why not take what was offered and just enjoy it? She was a gorgeous creature, in spite of her red hair.

And she must have had experience aplenty in how to please a man. Even before the death of her husband, an aging baronet, her lovers had been legion. Robert would not have thought twice, he could be sure of that.

"You do want me, Charles?" she whispered, pressing herself even closer against him. "Don't you?"

For a moment, Charles was tempted. After all, if she was not precisely the woman he wanted, was she not better than no woman at all?

But suddenly he felt sick, angry at himself. What was he thinking? In spite of her title, this woman was little better than a cheap whore. She had hurt Phoebe by her affair with Robert, and here she was trying to do the same thing again. But he was damned if he would allow Clarissa or anyone else to humiliate Phoebe She didn't deserve that! Not Phoebe.

Prying himself loose, Charles thrust Clarissa roughly from him and moved to the seat opposite. "For God's sake, Clarissa," he cried. "Try to remember that you are supposed to be a lady!"

He heard her gasp of surprise, and even in the dim light of the carriage he could make out the look of utter outrage on her face. It was not pretty. He wondered if any other man had ever rejected her so thoroughly.

"How dare you, sir?" Clarissa said, her whole body rigid with anger.

His composure regained, Charles spoke with his usual cool deliberation. "I would remind you, ma'am, that I am not my late cousin. Robert may have been fool enough to prefer you to Phoebe. But if you think I am so easily persuaded, you are sadly mistaken."

"So!" she said, her voice unnaturally high and crisp. "It seems that poor Phoebe has finally found someone so desperate that even she can satisfy him! In spite of all her talk, I knew it! You cannot be half the lover that Robert was!"

Ahah! Charles hardly knew whether to be amused or disgusted. Phoebe must have led Clarissa to believe that he was a great lover. Clarissa, in turn, had determined to find the truth for herself—and if she could wound Phoebe into the bargain, so much the better. It would serve Phoebe right if he succumbed to temptation. But no. He would not be used as a pawn in some capricious contest between two headstrong women.

Charles suspected that Clarissa had always secretly envied Phoebe. Phoebe was capable of real love, of genuine emotion, but Clarissa had only the instincts of an animal that satisfies its desires indiscriminately. He was not unacquainted with such females, but the thought of bedding this particular one revolted him. Still, he was a gentleman. There was no need to be deliberately cruel.

"You need not take this incident personally, Lady Stainford," he said. "You are a very attractive woman, and I'm sure many men would be happy to accept your most flattering offer." He paused a moment. "I'm afraid that you are just not the woman for me. But then, any woman would be a very poor substitute for Phoebe."

By this time they had traveled the very short distance to Clarissa's home and were pulling up before the entrance.

As she descended, Clarissa gave him a look of icy hatred. "You have caused me to make a fool of myself, which is something I cannot forgive. I suppose you and Phoebe planned this between you. But I never suspected you were such a fine actor. Mr. Kean is nothing to you, believe me!"

"I would escort you to your door," Charles said, ignoring this outburst, "but even my civility must end somewhere."

"You wanted Phoebe all along, didn't you?" she cried, turning to fire this parting shot. "Even while Robert was alive. You smug, self-righteous hypocrite! Well, the two of you deserve each other. I hope you will both be miserable!"

Having delivered this pettish speech, she flounced off, and Charles did not even wait to see her enter the house before instructing his coachman to drive on. He did not, however, go to Boodle's as he had planned. At the moment, he could not face his friends at the club. Clarissa's last words had had a more stunning effect on him than she could have guessed. He needed time to reflect, to face some very unpalatable facts.

For the next hour or more, Charles sat alone in his study, in total darkness, nursing a bottle of brandy. He had always prided himself on being able to keep his personal life well ordered. But this ugly incident forced him to re-examine himself—particularly his feelings for Phoebe—and what he discovered was as unsettling as it was unexpected.

Clarissa's accusations were far closer to the truth than he cared to admit. From their very first meeting, Phoebe Bridgerton had possessed the uncanny ability to provoke him in a way no other woman ever had. Over the years, she had inspired many emotions in him—disdain, frustration, and downright anger. But behind it all, he knew now, was something else—something hidden, something his conscious mind had continually and ruthlessly suppressed. And this newly discovered emotion was the most powerful and dangerous of all: desire.

Chapter Six

The sunlight streaming through Mrs. Comston's drawing room window the next morning was much too bright. Phoebe's tired eyes were smarting as she tried her best to avoid Mrs. Hargood's gaze. It was impossible, however, to avoid her distinctly articulated words.

"I declare, I scarcely recognized my own son!" Charles's mother said now, in a tone of hearty disapprobation.

Such an announcement was not at all what Phoebe needed to hear. She had spent a very restless night wondering and dreading whatever schemes Clarissa had hatched to entrap poor Charles. At last she had managed to convince herself that this was just an absurd coincidence, which she was exaggerating out of all proportion. And now here was Mrs. Hargood, promptly proving her worst fears to be fact. Charles had spent the evening flirting with Clarissa—yes, actually flirting! And the two of them had left the party together in his carriage. Phoebe felt that she was only now discovering the true meaning of misery.

"He has never spoken so abruptly to me before," Mrs. Hargood continued. "And I have never known him to flirt with any woman. Why, he does not pay half as much attention to you," she went on in an aggrieved tone, "as he did to Clarissa. And you are practically his wife!"

"Such behavior is not uncommon with husbands nowadays, I believe." Phoebe shrugged.

Mrs. Hargood squinted as if she could even now envision the painful scene. "I tell you,

Phoebe," she said, "the two of them were as thick as thieves last night. I did not know they were so well acquainted. Did you?"

Phoebe very carefully poured herself a cup of tea. "I did not. But perhaps neither of us knows Charles as well as we imagine."

"After last night, I no longer know what to think! Did you know, they lost every hand they played?"

Phoebe raised the cup and took a sip. "I suppose, then, that their opponents were sorry to see them go. They must have won a tidy sum."

"But Charles almost never loses," his mother complained. "He is a very fine card player. If he had any taste for gaming, he could make a sizable fortune at the tables."

"His luck must have been out last night," Phoebe said. "Or perhaps his thoughts were occupied with matters other than cards." She wished that Mrs. Hargood would leave off this subject. But, torn between a desire to know every detail and a feeling that she could endure no more such revelations, she was unable to curb her own morbid curiosity.

Mrs. Hargood set her teacup down in its saucer with a loud clink. "Well, if my son must make such a cake of himself, I could wish it were over someone better than Clarissa. I would not have thought her at all the sort of woman to catch his fancy."

"She is very beautiful," Phoebe admitted, though it cost her something to do so.

"Hmmph!" Mrs. Hargood snorted. "So is a tiger. But I would not want to share a carriage with one."

Phoebe smiled somewhat sourly, "I think a man would not view Clarissa in quite the same light as you or I."

"I daresay. But I should be sorry to think that

Charles is as big a fool as most men."

Phoebe would be even more sorry to believe so. She, of all people, must know that gentlemen were no angels. But that did not mean there was no pain in learning that yet another man seemed to prefer the flashy redhead to herself. It was obvious that Charles did not find his future wife much to his liking, so it was not at all incredible that he should be attracted to some other lady. If only it had been someone else, she told herself—anyone else!—it would not have hurt half so much. She was slipping into as fine a state of self-pity as any woman ever enjoyed, but she could not seem to stop herself.

Letty's appearance at the door should have been a welcome diversion, but it proved exactly the reverse. She came from her mother's bedside, where she had been ministering to that good lady, who was prostrate with grief at the death of one of her oldest and most beloved pugs. Mrs. Hargood did not care about that. She proceeded to relate the whole of last night's escapade to Letty, so Phoebe was forced to listen to it yet again. She found it no more amusing the second time than she had the first. Letty, however, seemed enthralled by the tale, sitting with wide-open eyes throughout.

Phoebe truly loved Charles's mother, but it was one of the most blessed moments of her life when Mrs. Hargood finally said she must fly, she was promised to pay a visit to an old friend, whom she must not disappoint. Thank God, Phoebe thought, for old friends.

"How horrible!" Letty exclaimed as soon as the door had shut behind their guest. "And to think that only yesterday we were sure Charles would never behave so. Why, it seems that your second husband will be every bit as bad as your first."

Phoebe acquitted her friend of any desire to wound her intentionally, but this thoughtless remark was not designed to soothe already overset nerves. "For my part," she declared, "I do not wish to hear another word on the subject. In fact, if anyone so much as mentions either Charles or Clarissa to me, I shall scream!"

Even Letty could not mistake the tenor of this speech and wisely refrained from further comment. Watching Phoebe pacing up and down in obvious agitation, she ventured to ask instead if her friend would care to take a walk in Hyde Park. Phoebe, feeling that to remain confined to the house would only exasperate her more, eagerly accepted the offer. The weather was considerably warmer than it had been, and she had rather be up and doing something than sitting there dwelling all afternoon on events beyond her power to alter.

She put on a wide-brimmed straw bonnet, tied with a cherry-red riband, immediately feeling much more the thing. As they sauntered through the park together, the combination of passing scenery—even that of a dull March day—and Letty's continual flow of pleasantly silly chatter offered Phoebe some diversion to soothe her overwrought nerves.

But their companionable stroll was soon interrupted by the arrival of a familiar figure on a rather showy stallion.

"Good day, fair ladies," Douglas greeted them heartily. "Might a poor gentleman be permitted to escort such flowers of loveliness?"

"Your compliments are as ridiculous as your waistcoat," Phoebe said, eyeing his sartorial display with pained distaste.

Dismounting deftly, he hastened to defend himself. "I assure you, this outfit is the high kick of fashion."

"It is perfectly hideous, fashion or no. Those stripes must be an inch broad at least," Phoebe continued. "And that mount of yours is not worth whatever outrageous price I am sure you paid for him."

"Really, Phoebe," Douglas complained. "You begin to sound more like Charles Hargood every day."

Letty, probably hoping that this mention of Mr. Hargood would not bring on Phoebe's threatened scream, interjected hastily, "I think it is a perfectly splendid waistcoat, Lord Douglas."

"If you are pleased with it, Miss Comston, I need no approval from anyone else," he replied, giving Letty a look that set Phoebe's teeth quite on edge. Never, she thought viciously, had anyone so nearly resembled a lovesick cow. How she managed to hold her tongue and not tell him so, she did not know.

They walked on together for a few minutes, Douglas drawing smiles and laughs from Letitia several times as he chatted pleasantly and commented on the assortment of dandies, dowdies, and freaks they spied. But Phoebe was not amused.

"Oh!" Letty cried suddenly. "There is Pamela Anstey! Do pray excuse me a moment. I must speak with her." She darted off to her friend, leaving the other two alone for a few brief minutes.

"You are unusually quiet today, Phoebe," Douglas said.

"Would that I could say the same for you, Phoebe replied tartly. "If you keep running on in this inane way, you will have Letty convinced that you are the silliest rattle in London.

Douglas's brows drew together. "There is no need for you to rip up at me like this. Just because you are marrying that prosy fool, Charles, is no reason to be so waspish with everyone else."

"How dare you speak of Charles in such terms to me!"

This high-flown statement was too much for

said of him, I know not how many times!"

"That," she said grandly, "is quite different."

"Forgive me, Phoebe," he said, looking very concerned at her odd reactions. "I had no idea that your feelings for Charles had undergone such a change. If you do indeed care for him—"

Phoebe halted at once, turning on him like the wasp he had just called her. "I hope I am not such a fool as that!" she cut in indignantly. "You may be determined to act the nodcock over Letty, but not everyone is so afflicted."

"What has that man done to you?" Douglas cried in exasperation. "I have never seen you in such ill humor."

Realizing rather belatedly how ungracious her conduct must seem, Phoebe was sincerely sorry for it. She was unhappy enough, but that was no reason to punish poor Douglas. He was not responsible for her misfortune.

"I'm afraid it is you who must forgive me," she said, giving his arm a squeeze. "The truth is, I do not feel quite myself today. It must be the weather. That, however, is no excuse for my behavior."

More than willing to forget their quarrel, Douglas drew her arm through his. "It is your dissipated way of life, my dear," he teased. "Have I not always warned you of it? You stayed out too late last night, I'll wager. I only hope you do not lead poor Charles from the straight and narrow."

Phoebe smiled dutifully at this sally, feeling more dismal than ever. If Charles had been led astray, it was certainly not her doing. "What nonsense you talk," she said. "I left Almack's quite early, as it happens. And Charles, I suppose, was at his club."

"You are certainly out there, my girl!" he answered lightly. "Charles was not at Boodle's last night. I know, because I looked in myself, imme-

night. I know, because I looked in myself, immediately after leaving Almack's. I spent the night in the drawing room dreaming of my angel. And I never laid eyes on Charles."

He said no more, for his "angel" chose that moment to return to them. But for the rest of the day, and for many days after, Phoebe was able to think of nothing else. She had no idea what happened on the remainder of their walk, and scarcely noticed when Douglas bid them a reluctant farewell.

Without the least suspicion of having done so, Douglas had shattered Phoebe's last hope that Clarissa might not succeed in her designs on Charles.

Mrs. Hargood had said very definitely that Charles offered Clarissa a ride home on the way to his club. That was bad enough, for who knew what might have occurred between Mrs. Burchell's house and Lady Stainford's residence? But things now appeared infinitely worse. Charles had not gone to his club at all, and it required very little imagination to guess with whom and in what manner he had spent the remainder of the night.

Phoebe's spirits had never been so low. Had she confronted Charles with her suspicions, she might have been spared a great deal of discomfort. But such was the state of her emotions that she felt she needed no further proof of her rival's success.

She did not blame Charles. It would be a rare man indeed who did not succumb to Clarissa's charms. And the woman must have been at her most persuasive last night. Still, that made things no easier, for once again Phoebe was in the unenviable position of being second best. Not that she had expected Charles to play the lover. But neither had she harbored any suspicion that his affections might be engaged elsewhere. Irrational though it might be, she was hurt. How could she possibly contemplate marriage with a man who was secretly lusting after another woman?

Poor Charles. Phoebe was quite correct in believing him guilty of the most shocking feelings of lust. It would almost have been better for him if the object of that lust had been Clarissa. At least *she* would have been more willing to satisfy it. But to be almost crazed with desire for a woman who felt nothing for him but contempt! It was utterly mortifying.

Charles had not had a great deal of experience with women. As with many quiet people, his reserve masked a passionate, even sensual nature. But he was generally able, by sheer force of will, to keep that nature in subjection. On those rare occasions when he required the satisfaction of intimate relations with the opposite sex, there were houses where such pleasures could be obtained—for a price. He was tempted to return to one of those establishments now, but he knew it would not serve. Neither his conscience nor his heart would permit it.

He wanted Phoebe. But Phoebe was not one of the bits of muslin with whom he had infrequently indulged his more earthy appetites. She was a lady. When it came to the refined sensibilities of such a creature, he was woefully ignorant. With Olivia, no such misgivings had troubled him. After all, there had never been much danger of his emotions leading to any unseemly behavior.

As he became less and less able to control his feelings, Charles grew more and more ashamed of them. He even found himself regretting that he had not taken advantage of Phoebe that morning in his bedchamber at Camberley. She was no fool. Had she guessed that he was nude? If so, she must think him an absolute savage! But Charles found night shirts uncomfortable and confining and had long ago dispensed with them. Surely every man must be allowed some unconventional habit, especially one which was unknown to any but himself—and now, perhaps Phoebe!

Soon he and Phoebe would be husband and wife. They would be sharing the same house. The same bed. He presumed that she wanted children, as did he. That was what had finally pushed him to the point of offering for Olivia. So Phoebe must be aware that they would consummate this marplot marriage of theirs at some future date. But if she should ever guess just how eager he was to do so—and how little his eagerness had to do with producing an heir! No. He must be careful not to reveal his weakness to her. It would be disastrous.

For the moment his only solution seemed to be to avoid her altogether. But this was a temporary measure at best. As he was painfully aware, the wedding was a mere three days away. After that, he could not imagine what he was going to do.

Both Charles and Phoebe had reached the point where each was determined to keep out of the other's way. With two such strong-willed people, the success of their efforts was virtually guaranteed. Phoebe dreaded facing her betrothed, almost as if she expected the signs of his seduction to be imprinted on his countenance in vivid crimson. Charles, in turn, feared that he would betray his passion for her in some obvious and deplorable manner which he could not even begin to conceive.

In the end, it was not until they actually stood face to face before the bishop that Phoebe and Charles again set eyes on each other.

Chapter Seven

The day that Phoebe Bridgerton and Charles Hargood were united in the holy bonds of matrimony was a balmy day, aglow with the first sunny weather of a decidedly chill March. Letty declared that it was the beginning of spring, but Phoebe felt she was facing the winter of her discontent. She wore a gown of palest blue satin covered in delicate lilac-colored lace. As her only attendant, Letty was arrayed in virginal white.

Driving off to St. Giles's with Mrs. Comston in her stylish new landau, Phoebe was not looking forward to the ordeal ahead. But in the end, everything went so smoothly and was over so quickly that Phoebe could hardly believe it. When she walked up the aisle and first caught sight of Charles, she experienced a moment of acute embarrassment and a peculiar feeling of shyness. However, as they repeated their vows before the small group of well-wishers, she became gradually more at ease.

Here she was, she realized, committing the rest of her life to Charles Hargood. Only a month before, she would have laughed at the very idea and declared it ludicrous and impossible. Yet as she heard Charles's calm, even tones reciting the familiar phrases from the Prayer Book, it all seemed somehow inevitable.

Charles himself appeared quite impervious to the strangeness of the situation. He might have been doing this every day of his life, for all the agitation he displayed. His groomsman, Mr. Tilson, a tall, sallow-looking fellow, was much more nervous. Charles did look rather tired, though—as if he had not slept well the night before. He had probably been carousing with his cronies. Or had he been with someone else? Better not think about that!

Following the simple service, everyone repaired to the home of the bride and groom, where they were treated to a light but satisfying nuncheon.

Phoebe was most pleased, amid all the congratulatory remarks, to renew her acquaintance with Stephen Dodd. The squire had come down the evening before expressly to support his old friend Charles through this most trying exercise.

Phoebe had only met him once or twice before, but she very much liked his frank, unaffected manners and the look of humor in his gently twinkling blue eyes.

"It is truly a pleasure to see you again, Mrs. Hargood," the squire said, coming up to her as she stood for a brief moment alone.

Phoebe greeted him with her warmest smile. "I had much rather you call me Phoebe, sir," she said. "Charles's mother will always be Mrs. Hargood to me."

He laughed at this, but only replied, "Thank you, ma'am. And of course you must call me Stephen."

"Flirting with my wife already, Stephen?" Charles asked, commandeering Phoebe's arm as he joined them.

"Not at all," Stephen objected. "But did I not have a very pretty wife of my own at home, I should be sorely tempted."

"How does Emily go on?" Charles asked. "Forgive me for not inquiring after her before."

Stephen did not seem to mind his friend's oversight. "Emily is much improved, I thank you," he said. "And you are quite forgiven. A man is entitled to be forgetful on his wedding day, you know."

"Has your wife been ill, then?" Phoebe looked from one to the other. "Charles has said nothing of this to me."

"No, no," Stephen hastened to assure her. "It is merely that she has recently presented me with my very first daughter—after two stout sons! She is rather worn out, poor honey, but very pleased with herself. As well she should be."

Phoebe was quite put out at her ignorance and gave Charles what she hoped was a suitably reproachful look. "I must offer you my congratulations then," she said, "though it seems they are a little tardy."

"Well, we shall simply blame Charles for that, shan't we?" Stephen said wickedly. "But I am sure it will not be very long before I am congratulating the two of you on a similar happy event."

Since neither Charles nor Phoebe knew quite how to respond to this, each studiously avoided the other's gaze. But their embarrassment only seemed to amuse Stephen Dodd. He laughed heartily and said that he looked forward to seeing them at Camberley very soon, then asked whether there was to be a bridal trip.

"I did not think it necessary," Charles replied quickly, obviously glad of any other topic to discuss. "Perhaps next year, if all goes well, we may follow the fashionable into France."

Phoebe was surprised at such a concession from her husband. "What a splendid notion, Charles!" she cried. "I see that you are indeed a prince of husbands. I have never been to France. But every woman longs to visit Paris!"

"Then we must certainly go," Charles said, the picture of the indulgent spouse. "But I fear I must say of Paris what Johnson said of the Giant's Causeway. Though it may be worth seeing, it is hardly worth going to see!"

When Phoebe protested at this damping conclusion, and enlisted Stephen's help in challenging it, a lively debate ensued in which Charles's good sense was no match for Phoebe's enthusiasm.

The afternoon passed away most pleasantly. While they were surrounded by their friends, Phoebe felt very little uneasiness. The reality of her position had scarcely had time to impose itself upon her. As the day wore on, however, and the party began slowly to disperse, she was touched by the first faint glimmer of apprehension.

At last even Charles's mother had to leave. She was returning to Camberley, accompanied by Squire Dodd. A newly-wed couple, she declared, needed privacy to adjust to their situation. Phoebe, who did not share her mother-in-law's views, could not persuade her to remain.

Mrs. Hargood insisted that she had to make preparations for her removal from Camberley. "No house can stand two mistresses," she said with calm resolution. There was a large cottage on the other side of the park which, when properly refurbished, would be the very thing for her. She bid her son and daughter-in-law a smiling farewell and was led away by Stephen, who was impatient to return to his own hearth and increased family.

Phoebe and Charles were now left alone in their house. Apart from the butler, Phoebe's maid, Rebecca, and a few other servants, there was no company at all. For some moments after Mrs. Hargood's departure, they stood in subdued silence, both acutely uncomfortable.

The evening loomed ahead of them, an interminable time of mutual discomfort. Fortunately, Charles had foreseen this dilemma and had already arranged for them to attend the theater. When he rather hesitantly reminded his wife of this, she seized upon the opportunity to excuse herself by claiming—with some truth—that she must rest before their outing.

Safely in her room, Phoebe wondered how she was to endure what seemed to her the longest and most fatiguing day of her existence. She would have given a great deal to know what her husband was thinking. But perhaps for a man—and one with such a dearth of sensibility as Charles—a situation such as this was no great matter. Could she have known the nervous agitation which Charles was experiencing at that very moment, she would have been astonished.

It is a rare man indeed who does not feel some apprehension on his wedding night. In Charles's case, it was more trying than usual, for two very good reasons. First was the intensity of his desire to consummate his marriage, and second was the absolute necessity of suppressing that same desire. He wanted no unwilling woman in his bed, certainly. But would Phoebe ever come to him of her own accord? Would she ever choose to share his bed? And if not, how long would his honor hold out against his growing hunger for her?

~/~

They both were very well turned out for their evening's entertainment. Each politely complimented the other on their attire as they partook of an early supper before departing. Both showed an unusual degree of interest in the weather. And both were heartily relieved when their meal was ended and they could leave for the theater.

The play was Shakespeare's *Romeo and Juliet*. Never had Phoebe liked this play less and never had an evening passed so slowly. She and Charles were greeted by several acquaintances,who gave them knowing looks and were pleased to make a number of would-be-witty remarks concerning their choice of play.

At the end of the mediocre performance, Phoebe did not know whether she should rejoice at having at last escaped from public annoyance, or to regret that the most trying portion of the evening yet lay ahead of her.

"Could you not have chosen something more suitable for us tonight?" she snapped as they drove off in their carriage.

Charles was surprised. "I believed you were an admirer of Shakespeare."

Twisting the cord of her reticule in her fingers, Phoebe wished it were Charles's neck. "Who but a Frenchman could not admire Shakespeare?" she countered. "But of all plays to pick, this was surely the worst!"

Charles had removed his gloves and was quietly crushing them in his hands. "Forgive me," he said, his voice sounding strained even to his own ears. "I did not think—"

"Exactly!" she interrupted. "I hope you do not expect me to do all your thinking for you."

"I do not expect the impossible." He could hardly believe that she should choose this, of all times, to pick a quarrel. But if she wished it so, he was quite willing to oblige.

"Upon my word, Charles, you grow more provoking with every day that passes."

With such pleasant remarks they whiled away the journey home and only called a halt when the footman opened the carriage door for them to descend. It would certainly not do to expose themselves before their servants. The remainder of their quarrel must wait.

As they entered the house and made their way upstairs, Phoebe felt a return of all the nervous alarm she had experienced before the play. Their lively bickering had momentarily dispelled her anxiety, but now it rose with every step she took toward the top of the stairs. At last she could bear it no longer. When they reached the door to her bedchamber, she stopped abruptly.

"Well?" she said.

"I beg your pardon?" Charles appeared quite mystified.

"Do not be obtuse, Charles!" she returned, her sharpness masking a moment of real panic. "Are we to share a bed tonight, or not?" She felt she could have boxed his ears for the look of surprise on his face. It seemed he had never even considered the possibility.

"I think," her husband said slowly, "that we must give ourselves time to become a little more accustomed to our peculiar circumstances. We have both of us been under considerable strain in the past weeks. When we are more settled, it will be time enough to consider such matters."

"Indeed," Phoebe said, standing stiff as one of the pillars at St. Paul's.

"I believe," Charles continued with painful deliberation, "that I am right in thinking that we both want children. However, I am sure it is better not to rush into a situation which must be so awkward and disagreeable to us both."

"Good night then, sir," Phoebe said curtly. Without even waiting for his response, she turned immediately and slipped into her room.

Inside, with her back against the closed door, Phoebe felt a ridiculous sense of anticlimax. After all her worries, Charles had dismissed the entire issue with no more than a few prim phrases. What a cold fish he was—an unfeeling prig. Or perhaps he was not so cold where a certain person was concerned?

Phoebe would not even ring for Rebecca's assistance but struggled to undress herself while she raged inwardly. What was the use of putting off the inevitable? Better to have consummated this hateful marriage tonight and have done with it. Not that she wished for such a thing, of course. But at least he might have displayed a little more emotion—more unease or disappointment perhaps. After all, it was not as if they had never been in bed together before!

Her brows drawn together, she sat staring mutinously at the connecting door between Charles's bedchamber and her own. There was a faint sliver of light showing beneath it which, as she watched, suddenly went out. A moment later she heard the sound of booted feet pass by her door and disappear down the stairs. Charles had gone out.

Well, it would certainly not be necessary for her to lock the door between them! But where had the wretched man gone at this hour? Of course...! Why, the explanation was so obvious, she wondered that she had not thought of it before. He had gone to Clarissa.

No wonder he had been so reluctant to share a bed with his wife. Why should he, when he already had a woman who probably meant more to him than Phoebe ever would?

What was it he had said just now? That the consummation of their marriage would be disagreeable to them both? What he meant was that it would be abhorrent to him! Phoebe's self-esteem, which had been crushed by Robert, was now ground into the dust.

Never had she felt so terribly alone—not even when Robert had betrayed her exactly as Charles was now doing. It was not that she was disappointed. She did not want Charles Hargood. Still, she felt an unreasoning sense of hurt because it was so horribly plain that Charles did not want her. And there was no one to whom she could turn for comfort. Even her mother-in-law had deserted her. She was alone in this too quiet house.

Throwing herself down on the great bed,

Phoebe did something she had not done in years. She turned her face into the pillow and wept bitterly. But even as the tears soaked the linen, she vowed that Charles Hargood would not make a fool of her as his cousin had. She alternately raged in righteous anger and wept in hopeless self-pity, and it was quite late before she fell into a troubled and unrefreshing sleep.

~/~

Charles, meanwhile, slept quite as little as his wife, but not for the reasons suspected by Phoebe. Prey to the most savage frustration and abject misery he had ever known, he spent several hours walking the streets of London. He dared not stay at home, for the unlocked door to Phoebe's room was a temptation he was not at all sure he could withstand. Consequently, it was almost dawn before he stumbled home to his bed.

Neither he nor Phoebe was in the best of moods the following morning and scarcely spoke a word to each other beyond a few icily polite phrases. They might, Charles thought, have been strangers who met by chance at an inn.

Always a conscientious man, Charles passed the next fortnight in a sincere but futile effort not to want his wife. But he was well aware that it was only a matter of time before his good intentions and his usually excellent self-control deserted him.

Phoebe was not making things any easier for him either. The new Mrs. Hargood seemed to be enjoying the privileges of marriage to the hilt. Having been given a generous allowance by her husband, she indulged herself shamelessly. Her wardrobe was the most stylishly elegant of any woman in town, her bonnets all the crack. She made heads turn whenever she drove her new curricle in the park.

Phoebe was soon surrounded by a court of ardent young and not-so-young gentlemen vying for her favors. One man, however, was conspicuously absent from her charmed circle: her husband, Charles.

Charles, in fact, found himself in a most unenviable position. His wife's extravagance was vexatious enough, but this was not the worst of her offenses. Charles stood by in mute anguish while she titillated society with her blatant flirtations and other escapades. Sick with jealousy and injured pride, he strove to present a picture of calm unconcern to his acquaintances, but his patience dwindled with each day that passed.

The behavior of the newlyweds was providing the ton with quite as much gossip-fodder as their engagement had, if not more. Not that it was an unusual arrangement among the *beau monde* for husband and wife to lead separate lives, but many had expected more from this particular pair. They were hardly ever seen together. While Phoebe peacocked at balls, routs, and masquerades, introducing Letitia to all the most suitable members of polite society, Charles spent quiet evenings at his club or with his own intimate friends.

Two people in particular were not pleased by this course of events. One was Lord Douglas, and the other—rather surprisingly—was Letitia.

"Do you and Charles do nothing together?" Letty asked Phoebe one evening as they sat together between dances at yet another gay party.

"Nothing," Phoebe answered, thinking of the bed, which Charles still showed no interest in sharing with her. Then, realizing how disconsolate she sounded, she caught herself up sharply. "Why should we? You, of all people, must understand our situation."

Letty colored, but did not abandon the topic. "Of course, I knew it was not a love match," she said. "But I do think you might—might make an effort to spend more time with each other." She paused, drawing a deep breath as if about to make some momentous statement. "Perhaps you should not be always taking me to parties and such—or encouraging Lord Douglas to accompany us. It looks so—so odd, you know."

"'Pon rep!" Phoebe cried, plying her fan with rather more vigor than needed. "Next you will be accusing me of flirting with Douglas."

"Well, you do. Frequently. And not only with him either!"

Letitia seemed really annoyed, which only set Phoebe's back up all the more. "Do not be such a prude, Letty," she said. "What would you have me do? Hang upon Charles's arm every night? I'm sure he would not appreciate it any more than I. Such behavior is dreadfully *démodé*, in any case."

Their promising *tête-à-tête* was cut short by the arrival upon the scene of Douglas himself. For this, Phoebe was most grateful. She did not relish being censured by a chit of a girl, friend or not—especially when she had precious little to say in her own defense. But Phoebe was not to be let off so easily. No sooner had Letty waltzed away in the arms of a handsome young officer than Douglas treated Phoebe to another helping of the same sauce. He was much more forthright, however.

"Really, Phoebe!" he said when she had sent one of her admirers trotting off in search of a glass of punch for his goddess. "Must you encourage that besotted sprig?"

"Jealous?" she said archly.

"Not at all," he returned. "But your antics are fast becoming the talk of the *ton*, my dear."

Phoebe dismissed the *ton* with a single contemptuous wave of the hand. "I pity my acquaintances, then," she said. "Their lives must be intolerably dull if they can find nothing more amusing to do than to talk about me."

"Forgive me," he said, fixing her with an uncompromising stare. "But you seem very eager to give them something to talk about. This Captain Dolan fellow, for instance. Not at all the thing, my dear, I assure you."

This reference to her latest conquest was not the most tactful one. Phoebe's temper flared. "Whom I choose for a friend is no concern of yours, Douglas! I live to please myself. If others do not like it, that is their misfortune—not mine."

"And your husband?" he asked.

"Charles?" she said, with a laugh which sounded brittle, even to her own ears. "I dare say he would not care if I ran off with one of the stablehands tonight."

"If you truly believe that," Douglas said, rising to take his leave, "then I do not think you know Charles Hargood very well."

He bid her good evening with a stiff little bow and left her to her own reflections. These were miserable enough companions, for Phoebe was confused and upset by her emotions and unwilling to look too closely into the reasons behind her outrageous conduct of late.

She felt a stab of pain somewhere in her breast which was becoming all too familiar. If only Douglas were correct.

If only Charles cared about what she did! And why should it matter to her, after all? Charles was an infernal nuisance, was he not? Yet his continued indifference was a source of constant irritation to her. She was determined to crack that pompous and coldly reserved exterior of his and to find out what lay behind it. But how? Oh, it was all such a hopeless predicament!

Chapter Eight

Descending the hall staircase in her new purple domino, Phoebe was well aware that Charles would not approve of her latest scheme. That was, of course, its chief charm. Had it been perfectly respectable and acceptable to her husband, she would not even have considered it. But Bagnigge Wells was a place upon which more fastidious persons tended to frown. Phoebe had certainly never been there, and until Captain Dolan told her of the masquerade to be held in the gardens that evening, had never felt the least curiosity about it.

Once the idea had been presented to her, however, she perceived immediately that it was a golden opportunity to vex Charles. The Captain had mentioned the affair only in passing, but was not at all displeased when Phoebe seized upon it with unexpected fervor.

"Oh, how I should love to see the gardens!" she exclaimed untruthfully. "And I so adore a masquerade ball! But my husband is so old-fashioned I fear he would never approve of my going." In truth, her husband would approve even less of her *cicisbeo*, for the Captain was not of the first respectability—or even the second. It was perfect.

Captain Dolan was eager to sympathize with her on her husband's lamentable character, to press her hand too hard and express rather too warmly his heartfelt desire to please her in every way. The rest was almost too easy.

In a remarkably short space of time, Phoebe maneuvered him into suggesting a clandestine rendezvous. "We shall have a grand romp!" he said with an over-hearty laugh. "I'm only surprised you haven't been to Bagnigge before. I was there last month with some friends and it was dashed amusing—'pon my word!"

Phoebe wondered if she would be able to endure an entire evening in this man's company. She had not at first meant to encourage such an overbold gentleman. He was handsome enough, though not at all in her style—too florid and too loud. But he was proving invaluable in her endeavor, for nothing could be more likely to enrage Charles than her association with such a mushroom. Indeed, Charles had already given her a hint in that direction.

Phoebe intended that night to be her crowning achievement: the pinnacle of vulgar provocation. Charles was dining out yet again, with one of his cronies, while she had excused herself from a similar engagement with Letty by pleading a sick headache.

As soon as Charles quit the house, however, Phoebe donned her costume and penned a brief epistle designed to make her husband mad as fire. If he should return very late, of course, her plan would be ruined. But he had been surprisingly concerned earlier by her feigned indisposition, and had promised to look in on her at a reasonable hour. She was gambling on his dependability and felt perfectly assured of ultimate success.

Captain Dolan arrived a few minutes late, in high spirits and eager for the treat in store. He was dressed as a court jester of old, in a motley outfit of red, green, and gold with a grotesquely tasseled cap. Phoebe, beneath her voluminous domino, was a flimsily attired Cleopatra. Her headpiece, however, was quite as odd as her escort's: a gilded tiara of intertwined serpents supporting a large gold disc above her brow.

After a seemingly interminable ride in a decidedly musty carriage, during which Phoebe was fully occupied trying to avoid the Captain's eel-like arms, they arrived at the pleasure gardens. Phoebe exited the conveyance with indecent haste, while her partner half stepped and half fell out behind her.

Upon entering the Long Room, they were presented with a wild clash of gyrating colors from hundreds of costumes of every description—from the frivolous and fantastic to the downright foolish. There was a great deal of noise and chatter, and loud music which seemed to be coming from an organ at one end of the room.

The Captain, in between attempts to discover the identities of the various masked revelers, pointed out to Phoebe the famous bust which adorned a niche in the wall. It was said to be that of Nell Gwynne, but Phoebe was doubtful. She could see nothing in the carved features which would have been likely to attract either king or commoner.

Pushing and squeezing their way through the crowd to the opposite side of the room, they were treated to raucous laughter and high-pitched squeals. The source of this mirth seemed to be a mirror which reflected a most unflattering image of whoever stood before it. Indeed, Phoebe found herself confronting a very portly Cleopatra, which Captain Dolan seemed to find most amusing.

Phoebe suspected that her escort had been a trifle disguised even before he arrived at her house. He was surely imbibing a good deal of scarcely potable wine now, and was well on the road to being completely castaway.

Thankful that her elaborate feathered mask preserved her anonymity, Phoebe was already heartily sorry that she had come. Not that any of her particular friends were likely to be present at such a gathering, but still, it was extremely uncomfortable. This was too high a price to pay, even for the pleasure of a fight with Charles.

She had no desire now to explore the outdoor paths. Her one wish was to get away as quickly as possible. She had intended to return home at a ridiculously late hour, but she felt that she had been here quite long enough. She must think of some other scheme to tease Charles. There was a note of genuine distress in her voice when she at last addressed Captain Dolan.

"I am not feeling at all well, sir," she said. "I fear I must go home."

But the Captain was in no mood to be denied his promised pleasure. "What!" he cried. "So shoo—so soon, Phoebe? I thought we might find a little—a little arbor in the garden later…"

"I really cannot stay," she began more forcefully, glad that she had had the sense to remain safely inside. "If you would be so good—" She stopped short when a large hand closed like a vice upon her shoulder. Turning sharply to protest this outrageous assault upon her person, Phoebe was amazed to behold not some bold buck or scoundrel, but her own husband.

In his austere evening dress, unmasked and obviously unimpressed by his surroundings, Phoebe thought Charles looked peculiarly out of place. At the same time, he made everyone else in the room appear silly and overdressed. So might Moses have looked among the heathens at Pharaoh's court.

"If you wish to leave, ma'am," he said in an expressionless voice, as Phoebe seemed incapable of further speech, "it would be my pleasure to escort you."

Captain Dolan was inclined to be indignant at this officious intervention. "And who—who might you be, s-sir?" he asked in an alarmingly belligerent manner. "This lady is with me! I shall take her ho-home myshelf."

"Mrs. Hargood happens to be my wife," Charles said, his manner unchanged. "So I believe the privilege must be mine."

This unexpected development threw the Captain quite off stride. "You're Phoebe's hus-husband?" he cried. "The devil!"

"Not quite," Charles answered. "But I am more than willing to introduce you to him."

Captain Dolan wilted where he stood and began to stammer something which might have been an apology, but Charles did not appear to consider it worth hearing. Without even a nod to the officer, he stalked off, propelling Phoebe inexorably before him. Many revelers turned to stare at the stern-faced gentleman and his Egyptian captive as they swept from the room so hastily.

Whatever Phoebe had expected, it was certainly not this. Her plan had succeeded beyond her most vivid imaginings. She had fully expected Charles to be waiting for her when she returned home, but that he should actually come in search of her was incredible. He was obviously furious. It could not be better!

Charles had not said one word since they deserted Captain Dolan. Phoebe was itching to speak but knew that she had better wait until they could be private. His gig was waiting outside. He deposited her in it none too gently before getting in himself and taking the reins. They pulled away as if pursued by the devil, and it was only then that Phoebe ventured to break the pregnant silence.

"What on earth brought you here tonight, Charles?"

He looked at her as if she had just asked if Prinny really wore a corset. "You have no idea, of course," he mocked. "The charming note which you left for me could not have been responsible for my presence."

She shrugged slightly. "Well," she said, "I really do not see why you should be so upset about it."

"Do you not?"

"Not at all. I merely went to a party with a friend."

"A friend," he said, pouncing upon the last word, "whose acquaintance you had been expressly warned against encouraging."

Phoebe fetched a world-weary sigh. "I knew you did not approve of the connection," she admitted. "But it was most unfair of you, Charles. You never even met Captain Dolan until tonight."

"True," Charles said, quite unmoved by this reasonable answer. "But though our meeting tonight was brief, it was more than enough to confirm my worst fears concerning his character and conduct."

Phoebe attempted to rearrange her headpiece, which had somehow been knocked askew. "It was not a fortuitous encounter," she acknowledged. "But the masquerade was such a lively affair any man should be forgiven for overindulging a trifle—"

"He was foxed," Charles said flatly. "Though I doubt that I would have thought him any more congenial had he been sober. It is not *his* behavior which concerns me, however."

Phoebe tilted her chin defiantly. "Am I now to be branded a loose woman because I went to a masquerade?"

"It was not a fit place for you to be," Charles said austerely. "Nor was Captain Dolan a suitable companion—for you or any other lady of quality."

"Really, Charles," Phoebe complained. "You sound more like your odious sister every day."

This remark was most successful in fanning the flames of Charles's wrath. He took a corner at a dangerously fast pace. "Do not attempt to turn the subject, Phoebe," he said. "My sister has no bearing on this matter. It was not my sister who deceived me tonight."

Phoebe was all injured innocence. "Deceived you?" she asked.

"Your famous headache, ma'am," he elucidated.

"But surely my note explained that I was feeling better and had decided to accept Captain Dolan's invitation? What is so remarkable about that?"

"The speed of your recovery must have been nothing short of miraculous!"

Phoebe sniffed loudly at this sneer. "You obviously do not believe me."

His gaze remained fixed on the road ahead, but his voice was harder and more chilling than Phoebe had ever heard it. "Let us say that I am not quite the fool you appear to think me," he replied. "I had been gone scarcely an hour when I returned to see how you were feeling. After leaving you—as I believed—almost insensible from pain, I expected to find you asleep, or perhaps only a little more comfortable. Instead, I discovered that you had gone out to a place of less than savory reputation—and with that thatch-gallows you refer to as a friend! It was only then that I recalled your ability as an actress and understood how thoroughly I had been duped."

Phoebe took care not to reveal her growing sense of triumph. "So," she said in pretended outrage, "you set out to drag me back home—by force, if need be, I suppose!"

"If I took a strap to you, it would be no more than you deserved."

Phoebe thought it best not to argue this particular point. "How did you recognize me in that crowd?" she asked instead, genuinely curious. "I was masked, after all, and I am sure you had never seen my costume before."

"I am perfectly capable of recognizing your figure, my dear," he said sardonically. "Especially when it is so amply displayed."

"You have quite spoilt my evening." She pouted. "I was having a lovely time before you arrived."

"From what I overheard, you were eager enough to go."

"It would have served you right if I had refused to come away with you."

Charles's face and voice were equally impassive. "It would have made little difference," he said. "You would have come with me—one way or another."

Phoebe was secretly rather impressed by her husband's manner. He was so cool, yet so forceful! But this was no time to abandon her charade. "I think Captain Dolan might have had something to say to that" she said, tilting her head the better to observe his response.

"If you think he could have stopped me, you are much mistaken," Charles answered with unimpaired confidence. "I have beaten bigger men in my time, and in his condition he could have been floored by an infant. Besides which," he added, "the Captain was under a grave disadvantage. He is not your husband. I am."

"In name only," she said scornfully.

"That," he said with quiet determination, "is something which can easily be remedied."

The breath caught in Phoebe's throat and she pressed her hand to it instinctively, as if to catch the air before it escaped completely. "What—what do you mean?" she stammered at last.

"Surely it is obvious," Charles returned coolly. "The present state of affairs could not continue indefinitely. It is time, my dear Phoebe, that you fulfilled your duty as a wife."

"But—but—"

"You seem to have forgotten, Madam, that you now have a husband. After tonight," he added deliberately, "you will not find that fact so easy to forget."

~/~

When they reached the house, Phoebe went quickly to her room. She cast aside her domino, took off the heavy tiara and ornate jewelry, untied her sandals and sat down upon the bed, clad only in the thin white sheath of her Egyptian gown. Though she had not had very much to drink, she felt strangely dizzy.

Charles had said not one word more on the subject, but Phoebe knew that he was not a man who spoke lightly of such matters. His words had been no idle threat—of that she was sure. Very soon now, he would join her in this very room and claim the rights of a husband.

It was not the unexpected announcement of his intentions, however, which had shocked her into an unnatural silence. Rather, it was the sudden realization that her whole campaign of teasing and tormenting her husband had been directed toward precisely this end. This was what she had wanted all along!

Phoebe, as a widow, was no stranger to the more intimate side of marriage. She had even enjoyed that aspect of it. But not even on her first wedding night, as a young and innocent bride, had she felt so nervous and uncertain.

She also felt—she could not deny it—the most exquisite degree of anticipation.

She tried to tell herself that it was a natural, if not entirely respectable, curiosity. Of course she wanted to know what kind of lover her husband was—and she could hardly ask Clarissa! But something told her that there might be much more to it than that. After all, she had known men far more handsome than Charles, who had never inspired in her the smallest degree of interest in their amorous abilities.

But since that startling morning when she had turned over to find Charles in bed beside her and knew that mad impulse to reach out and touch him, everything had changed. She wondered now, if she had given into that impulse, whether the scene Letty had interrupted would have been quite so innocent …

Phoebe put up her hands to cover cheeks which she knew must be a flaming red. It was thus that Charles discovered her when he softly entered the room. Perceiving that she was no longer alone, Phoebe stood up quickly to stare at her husband, her hands now clasped tightly before her. He had changed his formal coat and pantaloons and was attired in a brocaded dressing gown.

"I—I have not yet removed my costume," she faltered, feeling very silly for stating the obvious. An absurd shyness had taken hold of her and she dared not look directly at him.

"Let me assist you," he said, coming slowly toward her. Her head jerked up at this and her eyes encountered his. His tone, his movements were so controlled and composed. Yet his eyes seemed darker than usual, and his hands on her bare shoulders were surprisingly warm.

Phoebe was as stiff and unresponsive as a wooden post, and Charles was terribly awkward as he bent hesitantly to touch her lips with his own. That first kiss was not very encouraging. But as he followed it with another and firmer one, Phoebe's lips parted obligingly. This time the kiss was more like the one he had given her at breakfast that morning at Camberley. Only now there was no quick withdrawal. Instead, it went on and on, and ended only to be succeeded by a still deeper one.

At the same time, Charles had somehow managed to unfasten her dress, which fell unheeded to the floor. As he discarded the last of her garments, his hands began a slow and deliciously exciting exploration of her body.

Phoebe, meanwhile, had discovered that the only thing beneath Charles's robe was Charles. The robe consequently joined her forgotten gown as she learned at last the delights which her husband's body held in store.

By the time Charles lay down with her upon the bed, Phoebe had already decided that tonight was going to be the most wonderful of her entire life. But there was still more. The feel of him there beside her, the taste of his flesh upon her lips, was so good…his hands were everywhere, evoking a frenzy of desire within her that she had never before dreamed of…and where his hands led, his lips followed.

He besieged her senses with a fierce onslaught of passion, and when at last he took full possession of his newly-claimed dominion, the victory was as much hers as his. She tried to speak, to pray—to pray that this moment would never end. She knew that she gasped his name, for he seemed to be the only reality now, but beyond that she did not know what she said.

She might have known that whatever Charles Hargood did, he would do thoroughly—including pleasuring his wife. Phoebe even wondered briefly if it were possible for someone to die from too much pleasure—a surfeit of sweet sensation—then abandoned any attempt to understand or explain this incredible phenomenon.

This was no time for thinking. This was a time to feel. And what she was feeling now was absolutely glorious!

Chapter Nine

Charles Hargood could not sleep. Indeed, he wondered if he would ever know the meaning of rest again. Incredibly, Phoebe had fallen almost at once into the deep, untroubled slumber of a child. She lay snugly beside him, her breasts rising and falling in a gentle, even rhythm—the picture of tranquil contentment. But Charles knew how false that picture must be.

"What have I done? What have I done?" his mind repeated stupidly, over and over again. What had he done? He had made love to his wife! No. It was much more than that. He could not ease his conscience with pretty phrases. He had forced himself upon her—had ravished an unwilling woman. It was the act of a brute animal—not a gentleman.

The fact that Phoebe was his wife made it no better for him. True, she had not resisted him. She had submitted to his attentions—however reluctantly. There were even moments when he could have sworn that her pleasure was as great as his own. Perhaps—hateful thought!—she had been imagining that he was Robert.

She was too damned beautiful. That was the trouble. Looking down at her once more, he felt desire surge through him like a rising flood. Dear God! If he did not get out of this bed now, no amount of remorse and no tattered remnant of honor would keep him from taking her again.

He felt sickened at his own weakness. At this moment, all he wanted to do was to crush her soft mouth with his kisses, to lose himself in the sheer loveliness of her.

He had meant to be so cool, too—so restrained. It was all intended to exhibit his authority and to teach her what a wife's duty was. Besides, they had both always meant the marriage to be a real one—if only for the sake of children. But one taste of Phoebe's lips had ignited his passion like a spark in a powder keg.

What she must think of him now! What revulsion she must feel! After the finesse of an accomplished lover like Robert, to be subjected to his own rough and uncouth advances—so unbridled and uninhibited—must have filled her with horror.

Summoning his wounded pride and the last faint vestige of common sense, Charles eased himself gently out of bed, taking care not to awaken his sleeping princess. Separating himself from her was an exquisite torture. He could still feel the warmth of her body all down his left side as he retrieved his robe and slipped reluctantly into it. One last long look at her sleeping form, and he left the room as quickly as possible.

If only she had not gone off with that confounded Captain Dolan! When Charles had returned home earlier, worried that she might be really ill, to find what a gudgeon she had made of him, his fury had erupted with the force of a volcano. Until then, he had heard only enough about Captain Dolan to be suspicious of him. But as soon as he read Phoebe's terse note, Charles was filled with a wholly unreasonable desire to strangle a man whom he had never even seen.

He was jealous—insanely so. Phoebe's indifference to him was painful enough, but her defection with a man so decidedly beneath her was unendurable. Charles had known he would never rest until he found her and brought her home—to bed. But as he drove through the night to Bagnigge Wells, his temper cooled a little and gave him pause for consideration.

There was absolutely no need for Phoebe to have told him in her note where she had gone and with whom. The minx had wanted to make him angry. It was all just another scheme of hers to antagonize and humiliate her husband. Why, he'd wager that the unfortunate Captain was no more to her than a convenient tool for her purpose. Well, if she had meant to make Charles Hargood angry, she had certainly gotten more than she bargained for!

"Charles…please…" she had cried at one point last night. He had heard her breathless plea, but—God help him!—he was too far gone to heed it. So near to possessing what he had wanted for so long, he could not draw back. He had only stopped her mouth with his and pressed her deeper into the big, soft bed…

If she had despised him before, he dared not think what her opinion of him must be now. Yet he could have her again if he wanted. She could hardly object, having once capitulated.

But that was no use. He wanted no prim resignation, no icy martyr in his bed—a woman who endured what she could not enjoy. With all the unreasoning hunger of love, he needed to know that she wanted him as much as he wanted her. Nothing else would be enough. And that, of course, was quite impossible. She could never feel that way for him.

She must be aware now that he desired her—that she had at least that power over him. His feelings had been exposed for her to scorn afresh. Did the knowledge bring her any satisfaction, however bitter? Or did it merely add to her fear and disgust?

Perhaps she even pitied him! He could not bear that. He hardly knew now if he was more ashamed at having taken advantage of her weakness or having revealed his own.

In any case, there was no undoing the wrong he had done. His only hope of healing the damage was to give Phoebe a chance to recover without fear of another such incident. Perhaps, in time, she would understand and forgive. But first there was the small matter of an apology. Going to the elegant little *escritoire* in the corner, he sat down and extracted a sheet of paper from the drawer. Then he began the unenviable task of asking pardon for the unpardonable.

~/~

Phoebe slept late the following morning. When her eyelids finally fluttered open, it was to a strange sense that something was missing. Still half asleep, she struggled to grasp the elusive memory until, turning over, she spied the distinct indentation in the pillow beside her. Now she knew what was wrong. Charles was gone.

Of course. She ought to have remembered his odd, unfashionable habit of rising early. At least he might have kissed her good morning before leaving. But then, she would never have let him get away with just one kiss.

With a little sigh of supreme self-satisfaction, she snuggled under the covers and let her thoughts drift back to last night. What a night it had been! The first part of the evening had been nothing to crow over, what with the annoying squeeze of Bagnigge and the unwelcome attentions of Captain Dolan. But the time spent alone with her husband had more than atoned for that.

Closing her eyes, Phoebe could almost feel again the mesmeric rhythm of his hands on her back, the fiery trail of his lips across her breast, the muscled hardness of his thighs. Oh, why the devil wasn't he here when she wanted him! Her very fingers tingled at the prospect of running through his crisply curling dark hair, of stroking his broad shoulders, exploring the firm contours of his chest ...

Phoebe shook her head as if to clear it of the wild fancies which had sprung up so unexpectedly. She hardly knew which was more amazing: the incredible feelings which possessed her, or the fact that it was Charles Hargood who had aroused them. Charles. The biggest bore in England and—as she had so recently discovered—the most wonderful lover.

Comparisons are odious and unfair, of course. Still, it was impossible for Phoebe not to think of Robert at this moment. After all, he was the only other lover she had ever known, and she had never had any reason to question the general opinion that he was a most accomplished one. But until last night, there had been nothing to compare him to. The conclusion which she now reached was as startling as it was undeniable.

Robert's lovemaking had been rather like dancing a minuet. Every move was polished, practiced, and expertly executed. It had been very pleasant, but there was a curious detachment about it all. Robert always seemed too concerned with demonstrating to himself and his partner that his technique was impeccable. The pleasure of the dance was almost secondary. Then too, it did not appear to matter very much to him with whom he danced, so long as they got the steps right. He certainly changed partners often enough.

With Charles, it was more like waltzing—intimate, exhilarating and perhaps not quite respectable. What Charles lacked in finesse, he made up for in enthusiasm. He did not try to prove anything to himself or anyone else, nor did he need to. There was no practiced art to his movements; they came as naturally to him as breathing.

There was no doubt in Phoebe's mind which

she preferred. A waltz was much more enjoyable than a minuet. Charles was a capital waltzer, and the pleasure he received from it, he gave back to his partner in full measure. She felt, too, that Charles would be more fastidious in his choice of partner. She could hardly wait until the next set.

"You are positively addled, my girl!" Phoebe admonished herself. "Such thoughts are not at all seemly. They are the ravings of a wanton woman." Well, she was wanton—at least where her husband was concerned.

She wondered if he would come to her room tonight. He might be a little embarrassed. Indeed, she hardly knew how she was to face him herself. Yes, he would come to her, she was sure of it. If he had enjoyed last night even half as much as she had, he could not stay away.

Phoebe recalled how she had baited Clarissa that day at Madame Vidal's by hinting that Charles was a more satisfying lover than Robert had been. She could not have guessed then how accurate her assertion was.

But the very thought of that witch, Clarissa, irritated her. Resolving to forget her rival, Phoebe sat up and prepared to ring for Rebecca to help her with her toilet.

It was then that she saw the letter propped up on the small table beside her bed.

Phoebe knew at once, with absolute certainty, that it was not good news. It fairly shouted, "Disaster!" Her name was inscribed upon it in Charles's clear, clean script.

"Perhaps," she thought hopefully, "it is a love note." But that did not seem at all likely. Charles was not the sort of man to indulge in such sentimental whims. On the other hand, the Charles she had lain with last night was not at all the man she had thought she knew.

Gingerly reaching across, she took the neatly

folded paper in her hands and broke the seal. But whatever her imagination might have conjured up, nothing could have prepared her for the contents of Charles's terse note.

Phoebe, it began—very coldly, it seemed to her.

I wish to assure you that you need not fear any repetition of my behavior last night. It was a terrible mistake, which I can never sufficiently regret. In time, perhaps, it can be forgotten, and even though affection may be impossible between us, I shall hope someday to regain at least a degree of respect.

I believe it would be better for us to be apart for a time. I am returning at once to Camberley. It shall be entirely your decision as to when you wish to join me there. Your own feelings must be your guide.

Until then, please believe that if there were any way possible to blot out the shameful memory of last night, I would. I can only pray that time may yet do what I cannot.

—Charles

For a long time, Phoebe stared at the words before her, but it required several readings before the painful truth penetrated her numbed mind. Charles had gone. He would not be sharing her bed tonight. He would not be coming back to her at all.

The whole world seemed to go dark then. Phoebe felt as though someone had died. She very much feared it might be herself.

She had been so certain that Charles would be eager to experience again the delights they had savored together. It had been so perfect—so splendidly beautiful! But apparently Charles did not feel that way at all. The memories, which to were so precious and lovely, meant nothing to him but regret.It was impossible. It could not be so.

Once again she returned to a minute perusal of his letter, but it was of no use. Every word only served to drive another nail into the coffin of her dear departed hopes.

It had all been "a terrible mistake." He wanted to blot out the "shameful memory." It was better for them "to be apart." The truth was bitterly apparent. While he had thrilled her to the deepest core of her being, she had failed abysmally to satisfy him. He preferred Clarissa after all.

Was she, Phoebe, incapable of pleasing a man? She had certainly failed with Robert—and now with Charles,too. Or was it that Clarissa was so captivating that no woman could hope to match her abilities in the art of love? Perhaps Charles had sought last night to break free of his infatuation for Lady Stainford in the arms of another woman—but had found it to be ultimately impossible.

Perhaps he had even imagined he was holding Clarissa in his arms. The thought made Phoebe feel physically ill. Yet, had she only dreamed it, or had he whispered her own name, Phoebe, as he held her afterward?

This thought brought another, less pleasant one, with it. Whatever he had said, she had certainly called *his* name. She blushed painfully at the memory.

"Charles...please..." she had cried, begging for the complete union she craved—the perfect fulfillment of the desire he had aroused in her. She had abandoned every vestige of pride and dignity, surrendering herself totally to him. And what had been his response?

"Affection...impossible between us..." she read, still staggered at the enormity of her loss.

Charles no longer even respected her. His letter frankly admitted it. Her behavior had not been what a gentleman generally expects of his wife, she supposed. But the strength of her emotions had been overwhelming. Her response had astonished even herself, and she had been powerless to control it. She had acted like a common strumpet, reveling indecently in these new-found sensations. Charles must have been appalled.

Now Phoebe's humiliation was complete. She had lost everything: her respect, her peace of mind, her hope. Clarissa had beaten her again, even more soundly than before. Feeling utterly defeated, Phoebe began to cry quietly. Tears were getting to be a bad habit. Nevertheless, she continued in this unprofitable occupation for some twenty minutes before she determined that it was a pitiful waste of time. Now, if she could make Clarissa weep, there might be some pleasure in that!

For a short while, Phoebe was able to comfort herself by devising fiendish methods of torture for her red-haired rival. She thought longingly of pulling out the hairs on Clarissa's head strand by strand, until she was as bald as a billiard ball; or of forcing her to eat sweets until she was so obese and shapeless that no man would look twice at her, except to scoff.

But it was useless, for no plan Phoebe might devise could get her what she most desired: her husband.

Her ruminations were interrupted at this point by the arrival of Rebecca, who came to inform her that Miss Comston was below stairs waiting to see her. Phoebe felt in no condition to be receiving visitors, even Letty, but decided that she had rather not give anyone cause to suspect how unhappy she was. Unhappy people were such bores—a mortal sin in a society bent on extracting the maximum of pleasure from life with the minimum of morality.

Forcing herself to speak crisply, in spite of her recent tears, Phoebe instructed the maid to tell Letitia that she would be down directly. Something in her voice must have betrayed her, however, for Rebecca seemed quite concerned.

"Are you feeling poorly, ma'am?" she asked.

"I am perfectly well!" Phoebe snapped. "Now do not stand there gawking like a ninnyhammer! Deliver my message to Miss Comston at once."

Almost as soon as she had spoken, Phoebe regretted her churlish attitude. Rebecca was a good girl and did not deserve such treatment. But there was no time to apologize, as Rebecca darted from the room to escape any further reprimand.

When she returned, Phoebe did, indeed, beg her pardon. But Rebecca, looking from her mistress to the unusually rumpled bed, assured her that she understood perfectly. This disclosure only increased Phoebe's confusion and was no help at all in preparing her to face her young friend.

In truth, this morning Phoebe dreaded having to endure Letty's youthful high spirits. How dared anyone else be happy, when she was so utterly miserable?

She allowed the silent Rebecca to help her into a gown. "What day is it?" she asked, unnerved by the girl's unusual reticence.

"Tuesday, the first of April, ma'am," Rebecca said, attempting to tame her mistress's unruly curls. "All Fool's Day!"

How appropriate, Phoebe thought, with a twist of her lip which was cruelly reflected in the mirror before her. There surely could not be a bigger fool in England today than she.

Chapter Ten

Phoebe had dressed with great care, choosing a very flattering lilac-colored morning dress and a lace cap with pretty matching ribbons, and prepared to do her best to conceal her blue-deviled condition. If she expected to confront a cheerful damsel, however, she was sadly disappointed. Going down to the sunny drawing room, prepared with her brightest and falsest smile, she discovered Letitia crouched on the sofa and weeping loudly into a much-crumpled lace handkerchief.

"Good Heavens!" Phoebe was startled into exclaiming. "What on earth do you have to cry over?"

"Oh Phoebe," Letty whimpered, rising up and flying to her friend's bosom like a wounded lark. Phoebe, forced by common courtesy to embrace her, was treated to a series of half-moaned phrases which were quite incomprehensible. If Letty was attempting an explanation of her plight, she was failing dismally.

"For goodness' sake, Letty," Phoebe said, scowling, "do stop your crying." Fine advice from someone who had just been behaving like a watering pot herself. But this was too preposterous. "Pull yourself together, or I shall be forced to shake you."

"My life is over!" Letty announced dramatically, and Phoebe, who had been thinking pretty much the same thing about her own situation, found herself curiously unsympathetic. Whatever Letitia's troubles might be, Phoebe was sure they could not compare with her own.

"Fustian!" she declared, pushing Letty unceremoniously into a chair. "You had better tell me what this farrago is all about. And no more hysterics."

Letty was not at all pleased by this brusque response to her lachrymose state. She looked at Phoebe reproachfully. "How can you be so unfeeling?" she complained. "I thought you were my friend—that you would understand. Can you not see that my heart is broken?"

"So it seems." What did Letty know about a broken heart?

Letty was so disgusted by her friend's insensibility that she actually forgot for a moment to cry. "Do you not care at all, Phoebe?" she asked. "You, of all people, must know what it is to be deceived—to be betrayed by a man!"

Was her pain so obvious, Phoebe wondered, that even a green girl like Letty could perceive it? Oh, of course, she was thinking of her marriage to Robert! Phoebe had all but forgotten him. "What are you talking about?" she asked at last, exasperated. "Who has betrayed you?"

Letty bent to retrieve a copy of the *Morning Post* which had been lying unnoticed on the floor. She thrust it at Phoebe, as though offering an asp to Cleopatra. "Read this!"

Phoebe dutifully looked down at the paper and, after a moment's perusal, read aloud what seemed to her the most likely entry. "Doctor Croft's Remarkable Revivifying Powder," she pronounced slowly. "Guaranteed to ease biliousness and all—"

"Not that!" her friend interrupted, snatching the paper from Phoebe's hand and turning the page until she found what she was seeking. "Now read that!" She proffered the periodical once more and pointed to the offensive paragraph. This time Phoebe, spying the correct phrases, had no difficulty in comprehending the cause of Letty's affliction.

"Well!" she said. "So that is it. 'The engagement of Mr. Henry Fernleigh to Miss Ellen McCandlish...the marriage to take place...'"

Letitia collapsed onto the sofa as if dealt a stunning blow, crying, "Stop! Stop! I cannot bear to hear it repeated."

Phoebe tossed aside the *Post* with a careless gesture. "So the love of your life is to marry another," she said. "It is hardly the end of the world."

This terse dismissal of her tragic fate was so heartless that Letty could only stare at Phoebe in patent astonishment. "But I shall never be happy again as long as I live!" she cried.

Phoebe remained unmoved. "Do not be absurd, Letty. It is high time you got over your infatuation with Mr. Fernleigh. He was a dreadful bore anyway, and I rejoice that he is now plaguing some other unfortunate female."

"How can you?" Letty cried, springing to the defence of her beloved. "He is the most noble, most—"

"Most fickle man alive," Phoebe concluded for her. "Has he not proved as much by offering for someone else?"

At first, Letitia could find nothing to say in reply to the manifest truth of this statement. Eventually, however, imagination came to her aid. "Perhaps," she ventured hopefully, "he has been forced into this by his wicked uncle. Or maybe he has been trapped by this woman against his will. Or—could it be that this is not my Henry at all, but some other gentleman—"

This was too much for Phoebe, who came to stand before Letitia and, grasping the girl's chin in her hand, forced her to cease her chatter and look up. "If you would stop confusing real life with the rantings of the Minerva Press, I would be excessively grateful," she said. Releasing Letty's chin, she continued crisply, "Henry does not love you. He has chosen instead to marry Miss McKintosh—"

"McCandlish," Letty corrected, sniffing ever so slightly.

"Whatever her name," Phoebe said, "she will soon be Mrs. Henry Fernleigh. And you, young miss, had better find yourself another man to fall in love with."

"I shall never love another!"

Phoebe could not help laughing at this impassioned outburst. How young Letty was, really. "In six months' time," she said, "if you can tell me that without smiling, I may even believe you."

Letty was inclined to take umbrage at this. She wiped away the last traces of her tears and glared up at Phoebe, saying crossly, "I do not know how you can mock my feelings so! If anyone could understand my feelings, I was sure it must be you. You have never fallen in love again, after all. Your marriage to Charles is purely one of convenience."

Was it? Phoebe wondered. She was not in love with Charles—at least, not if the giddy hero-worship she had felt for Robert was the standard by which to judge. She was not blind to Charles's faults, nor did she consider him to be the acme of perfection. Yet she had begun to entertain a certain grudging respect for him over the past few months, to appreciate his good sense and the basic kindness of his heart, which his occasional brusqueness could not entirely hide. In spite of everything, she knew in her deepest heart that she could have been truly happy with him—if it were not for Clarissa!

"That is beside the point," Phoebe said in answer to Letty's charge. "My case is quite different from yours. My marriage to Charles, for example, is an inescapable fact. Whereas your relationship with Henry was little more than wishful thinking."

"You think he never loved me?" Letty asked.

"To be truthful, I do not believe that you ever loved him."

This was too much for Letty, who looked as if she could not believe her own ears. "How can you say so?" she cried. "I have never loved anyone else!"

Phoebe became very serious now. "It is time to stop deluding yourself, Letty," she said. "I know all about that. As I told you before, Robert was not, in any way, the man my girlish fancy made him out to be." She held Letty's hands in her own and spoke with sincere conviction. "You are fortunate that you did not make the mistake of marrying your hero. Instead of lamenting your circumstances, you had better thank God for Miss McCandlish. She may have saved you from a most unpleasant fate."

The other girl appeared to have been calmed by this speech. "You do not believe that I would have been happy with Henry?" she asked.

"I do not!" Phoebe said emphatically, giving Letty's hand a reassuring squeeze. "Now, I suggest that you go home, rest, and reflect on what I have said. Tomorrow is Lady Sheltby's rout, and I see no reason why we should not both enjoy it."

Letty departed in a much more rational mood than when she had arrived. Phoebe had no doubt that the child would regain her *joie de vivre* very quickly. She was young, and her heart had not been as involved in the matter as she liked to believe. It was all more of a romantic conceit which had become a habit. Breaking that habit might prove painful, but the break would be complete. Even the Letitias of this world must grow up sometime.

If only my own troubles could be solved as

easily, Phoebe thought, despondently. But just as her feelings ran deeper than Letty's—she was not sure she wanted to know how deep—so her wounds would be a longer time healing. She was much afraid that she would never be quite the same as she had been before. Something truly momentous had occurred in her life, and its effects were only beginning to be felt. Why was it that Charles's passion had stirred her so deeply?

Phoebe was struggling to come to terms with her confused and contradictory emotions. She would have welcomed a period of solitude for this unusual exercise, but it was not granted. Letty had not been gone more than ten minutes when a second visitor was announced.

Douglas Ardshire was then admitted, and though he was not quite in the state of despair which possessed Letitia, he was obviously far from happy.

Not another one! Phoebe thought, most annoyed at having to receive him. But if her feelings were apparent in her voice or her apathetic reception, Douglas did not seem to notice anything amiss.

He muttered a brief "good morning," proceeded to pace about the room in some agitation, and finally burst out, "What am I to do, Phoebe?"

Phoebe managed to restrain the sudden urge to smash a lovely Sèvres vase over his very hard head. She had a good idea what this was all about, despite the cryptic nature of his words. Was she expected to console every lovesick nincompoop in the country? And who, pray tell, was to console her? Well, at least she need not make things too easy for Douglas. A little suffering would do him a world of good. Schooling herself to appear coldly polite, she asked, "What are you to do about what?"

"You must know how much I love Letitia!" he

declared, continuing his frantic pacing.

"Everyone from here to Botany Bay must be aware of that fact—with the possible exception of Letitia."

Douglas halted in mid-stride. "Exactly," he said. "She hardly seems aware of my existence."

"I am sure you exaggerate," Phoebe said with mock sympathy. "It is simply that your existence is a matter of small importance to her."

"How kind of you to point that out to me, Phoebe. I may now be at ease!"

Ignoring his sarcasm, Phoebe motioned for him to sit down. "For God's sake, Douglas, be still. I cannot bear to see you marching up and down like a misplaced dragoon."

He complied with this request, but very sullenly. "I do not know that I care to remain," he complained. "You are not much help. For all your talk of assisting me in my suit, I cannot get near Letitia."

"You danced with her two nights ago at Almack's," Phoebe protested. "And I am sure there are not many days when we do not run into you or when you are not escorting us to some *soirée* or other. You are forever at our heels, in fact."

"But I am no nearer to my goal."

Phoebe smoothed the skirt of her gown. "I can hardly be blamed for your lack of success in the way of courtship," she said. "This, I fear, is what comes of too many years of idle flirtations. You have lost the knack for inspiring a serious attachment."

"So I must study to be more sober," Douglas replied, clasping his hands together and resting his chin upon his knuckles. "Perhaps I ought to take lessons from Charles. After all, he succeeded in winning you when other men of considerable address had failed. Alas, I fear I am too frivolous!"

"Too old might be nearer the mark," Phoebe

retorted, as wounding a comment as she could muster. "You must be at least twelve years Letty's senior. No doubt she regards you as she would an uncle or some other elderly relation."

Instead of being enraged by this, Douglas appeared perfectly mortified. "Do you think so?" he asked in horrified accents. "I have never considered myself old, but it may be that to so young a girl—"

Even in the midst of her own misfortune, Phoebe could not help but smile at this sudden doubt on the part of one of London's most courted bachelors. "Do not be such a simpleton, Douglas," she said, deciding that he had suffered enough. "I was merely quizzing you. A man of your looks and address is just what most young girls dream of. Why, I know of several girls even younger than Letty who have developed decided *tendres* for you."

He did not seem particularly cheered by this, allowing his chin to sink even lower. "There is only one explanation, then," he said morosely. "For all my famed prowess in love, Letitia still prefers this Henry fellow."

Phoebe could see no hope for her own future, but there was no reason for denying Douglas what little was available to him. Someone had the right to happiness today, even if not herself. "If your despair is due to Henry Fernleigh," she said, "then I have some good news for you."

"What? Is he dead?"

The look of unholy relief on his face was almost enough to restore her own bruised spirits, but Phoebe permitted herself only a brief smile. "No, you unfeeling beast. He is not dead—for which you should be profoundly grateful. If he were, Letty would probably convert to Catholicism and enter the nearest nunnery, there to spend her life in romantic memories of her lost love." She fingered one earring, hesitating, with deliberate provocation, to make her revelation. "My news is far better than that."

"What good news is there," he said bitterly, "if he is not dead?"

Phoebe assumed an air of injured pride. "Do you doubt my powers, then? I have half a mind to leave you to your fate. You deserve no better."

Douglas looked up with something of his old humor in his eyes. "*Mea culpa*," he said. "But come. I know you would not withhold anything which could so materially affect my future happiness."

"Henry is to marry another!" she announced dramatically.

This simple statement worked powerfully upon Douglas. He stared at Phoebe in frozen silence for several seconds, before barking out, "Impossible!"

"On the contrary," Phoebe said, paying little heed to his incredulous exclamation. "Nothing could be more natural."

"What! To prefer some simpering female to Letitia?"

Phoebe gave him a withering look. "Your indignation, Douglas, is a credit to your heart but gives no very reassuring impression of your head. No one has a higher regard for Letty than I, but it is not at all likely that every man she meets will fall in love with her."

Douglas looked considerably abashed by this forthright speech. "Does Letitia know of this engagement?" he asked.

"It was Letty herself who informed me of it," Phoebe admitted placidly. "As might be expected, she is quite cut up by Henry's perfidy. She vows that she will never love again—or such was my understanding. She did not make much sense."

"If that is her mind," he said testily, "what good is all this to me?

Phoebe raised her eyes heavenward. "Deliver

me from the simplemindedness of men!" Redirecting her gaze to Douglas, she continued, "You cannot be such a buffle-head as to believe such protestations! Letty will soon recover from her megrims and will be ready to transfer her affections to a more suitable object."

"Such as myself?" he inquired as enlightenment dawned.

Crossing her arms, Phoebe contemplated him doubtfully. "If you make yourself available to comfort her," she said, "give her a manly shoulder to weep upon, and be generally agreeable—as you know well how to do—why not?"

"You think my chances are good?" he asked, looking engagingly boyish.

"My dear Douglas, nothing is more likely. Letty likes you very much already. The two of you always have your heads together, laughing and whispering."

He grinned saucily. "We are mostly whispering about you—especially since you've taken up with that Major What's-his-name."

Phoebe tossed her head at this, but merely said, "Then that is one thing you have in common already. You both disapprove of my conduct."

"You know, Charles ought to take a stick to you."

"Thank you."

Douglas laughed, the first really pleasant sound he had uttered since entering the room. "Where is Charles, by the way? I had hoped to speak with him about a new gun I wanted to purchase."

"To shoot yourself with, I trust," Phoebe snapped. "You seem eager enough to play Young Werther."

"You are the most vexatious woman," he declared with an impudent smile. "Charles has my deepest sympathy. But where is the wretched man?"

Phoebe looked down into her lap, not daring to meet Douglas's eyes. She did not want him to suspect her own secret heartache. There was no consolation he could provide. "Charles has gone down to Camberley," she informed him. "Some problem with the estate, I believe."

"Nothing serious, I trust?"

Nothing serious! Only the destruction of her happiness. Only the end of her dreams. "Oh no," she answered, quite pleased by her assumed insouciance. "I'm sure his bailiff could have taken care of it. But Charles prefers to attend to such matters himself."

"Perhaps he was running away from you," Douglas quizzed, never guessing the agony his words caused her. "If you treat him half as cruelly as you do me, I cannot say that I blame him."

~/~

Douglas soon left her alone. Phoebe was persuaded that he would eventually succeed in his courtship of Letitia. With a little perseverance on his part, she saw no reason why Douglas should not win her friend's heart.

But Douglas's questions about Charles had irked her considerably. He would not be the only one to remark her husband's absence so soon after the wedding. At least his interest had been mere friendly concern. Others, she knew, would not be so considerate, nor would they long refrain from inventing their own explanations—which would likely be far from complimentary.

Damn Charles! He had left her alone to bear the humiliation of being an abandoned wife. Well, she would not give him—or anyone—the satisfaction of knowing that his desertion had wounded her. She would laugh more loudly, flirt more gaily, and dance with more spirit than ever before.

No one would ever guess that she was the most miserable wretch in England. Instead, she would let it be plainly seen that her husband's departure was a matter of supreme unimportance to her. She would enjoy her season in London and forget all about Charles Hargood. The polite world might scorn her conduct, but she would not give them the pleasure of laughing at her behind her back. Let them laugh at Charles, if they liked! She would give them plenty of reasons to do so.

"You shall not boast that I am wearing the willow for you, Charles!" she vowed. And it was a vow she meant to keep.

Her one consolation was the thought that she might not, after all, be the biggest fool in London. She had strong competition from Letty and Douglas.

Chapter Eleven

For the first few weeks after Charles forsook her, Phoebe did an excellent job of ignoring his absence—at least in public. She was never still. Whether it was riding, waltzing, shopping or dining, she must always be doing something. The one thing she refused to do was to stay at home. Without Charles, the house was a cold, lonely castle haunted by the phantoms of her dead dreams.

Letitia frowned and Douglas lectured her for her never ending round of flirtations and assorted diversions, but Phoebe scorned their sensible advice. Let everyone feel sorry for Charles, if they liked. They would not pity her!

But her wild gyrations took their toll. As April retreated before the advance of a warm and fragrant May, it became harder and harder for Phoebe to keep up her frantic pace. She was not feeling at all well, particularly during the early part of the day, and she began to wonder if she could continue this pretence of enjoyment for the rest of the season. Even Letty was beginning to notice that something was amiss.

"Are you sure you are feeling quite well?" she asked one morning when she called to find Phoebe still abed long after she should have been out and about. "I do not at all like the way you are looking lately."

Phoebe hunched a shoulder. "Why not come right out and tell me that I am growing old and hagged, and be done with it."

"Now do not take such a pet, I beg! But anyone who knows you can tell that you are not your usual self."

Phoebe sat up straighter in the bed and squared her shoulders. "I was up too late last night," she explained. "That is all."

"You ought to rest more," Letty said sternly. "The way you are carrying on is scandalous, Phoebe. If Charles were to hear of it, I do not know what he would say."

"Perhaps you should write him a note." Phoebe's lip curled. "Send it by Douglas, if you like."

"That is not likely to be necessary. Your behavior is so blatant that I am sure news of it will reach Camberley without any effort on my part."

"I do not give a fig what Charles may or may not say. I shall live my life as I please—and he may go to the devil for all I care!"

Letty was clearly shocked at this unnecessarily vehement reaction. "You are his wife, Phoebe. I'm sure he would not approve—"

"What business is it of yours, in any case?" Phoebe interrupted rudely. "You are my friend—not my mother."

Letty rose from her seat beside the bed, and addressed Phoebe with immense dignity. "I am very glad that I am not your mother, Phoebe. If I were, I should be ashamed of my own child. And I am not even sure," she added, her chin high, "that I wish to be your friend any longer. If this is the way you treat all your friends, you will very soon find yourself alone in the world."

"Wait!" Phoebe cried, as Letty turned to make her departure. "Do not go, Letty! I did not mean it, my dear. It is only that I feel so wretched..." and, much to her own consternation, Phoebe began to cry.

In an instant Letty was beside her, eager to accept her apology. "Oh Phoebe!" she exclaimed, obviously distressed. "You must feel poorly, indeed, to behave so. I have never in my life seen you cry."

You have not been in my bedchamber every night when I retire, Phoebe thought bitterly. But aloud, she merely said, "It was unpardonable of me to take out my feelings on you. I am sorry, Letty."

Letitia was all concern now, Phoebe's insults forgotten. "Have you seen Dr. Langworth?" she inquired anxiously.

"No," Phoebe answered, her tears already dry. "I am certain it is nothing serious. A little rest, as you said, is all I need."

Letty put out a hand to feel her friend's brow. "You must stay at home tonight," she commanded.

Phoebe removed the hand and patted it gently. "I am not dying, I assure you," she said. "Besides, Douglas has promised to escort us to the Duke's ball tonight. And you have been so looking forward to it."

"Missing one ball will not kill me," Letty said with admirable fortitude.

"Nor will attending one carry me off," Phoebe answered firmly. "I shall rest tomorrow instead."

Letty began to debate the point but eventually acquiesced on the condition that Phoebe promise to attend no party or other amusement on the following evening. Only then did she consent to leave, warning Phoebe against any strenuous exercise.

Left alone, Phoebe's thoughts returned, as they so often did, to that last night with Charles. She had known even then that it was the most perfect night of her life. But perhaps it was even more momentous than she had imagined, for a new suspicion had taken hold of her in the past few days, a suspicion which was becoming stronger by the hour.

That night Charles had given her pleasure such

as she had never before known. But was it possible that he had given her even more? Could it be that, at this very moment, his child was growing within her?

For more than two years she had hoped and prayed that she might present Robert with an heir, but when no baby materialized she had concluded that she must be barren. But what if the fault had not been hers? She had never heard any rumor of Robert having fathered children by any of his numerous paramours. Perhaps he had been incapable of doing so. How ironic if that was the case!

But even so, was it likely that Charles could accomplish in just one night what Robert had not achieved in two years? Yes. When she recalled those blissful hours in Charles's arms, she could believe anything possible.

Getting out of the bed and going over to the cheval mirror which stood in one corner of the room, she surveyed her reflection from head to toe. She was looking a little pale and drawn, to be sure, but there was no other outward hint of any change within. Yet of late there were certain signs which indicated that the incredible had happened.

Once Phoebe had recoiled from the thought that Charles Hargood would be the father of her children. Now she was filled with a mixture of jubilant expectation and hopeless despair. It seemed that she had gained a child and lost a lover. The future was uncertain at best, but her prospects did not seem at all promising. In the meantime, there was a ball to attend and a crowd of people to deceive.

~/~

The Duke's home was one of the curiosities of London. Behind a rather austere Palladian facade, it boasted an entrance that was one of Robert

Adam's most spectacular designs, rivaling even that of 20 Portman Square. The grand staircase swept up in a broad spiral of gilt-edged grandeur. A dizzying array of bright-hued ornamentation attested to the nobility and wealth of its owner—a man, Phoebe reflected, who was often too castaway to find his way home unaided, and who was reputed to have recently lost the better part of his large fortune at the gaming tables.

Nonetheless, this ornate setting was the perfect stage upon which the dandies, diamonds, and dowagers of polite society might strut and parade before each other in smug self-satisfaction. Indeed, the sea of feathered turbans, glittering jewels, and richly-colored gowns almost dimmed the heroic brilliance of Mr. Adam's work.

Letty, ascending the stairs between Phoebe and Douglas, was awed into muteness. This pageant of domestic splendor was so impressive as to be oppressive.

"Have you ever seen anything like it?" she ventured, attempting to take in all the dazzlingly contrived artifice about her.

"Quite overwhelming," Phoebe agreed.

"Too damned fussy for me," Douglas said, viewing his surroundings with a practical man's disdain for artistic flights of fancy, and quite forgetting that his own ancestral home was scarcely less elaborate.

"Rich peers must be allowed their eccentricities," Phoebe said, pausing to inspect part of an intricate frieze. "I believe the present Duke's father was responsible for the decor. The library is said to be particularly fine."

They were soon able to ascertain the truth of this assertion as they inspected various apartments and were forced to admit that the library was very fine, indeed. Everything about the house was on a lavish scale, and Letty declared that she was sure the palace at Versailles could not boast anything finer.

In the course of the evening, they met numerous acquaintances. Phoebe, despite her problems, was not finding the outing unpleasant, and Letty and Douglas were plainly gratified to see her behaving with more propriety than she had of late displayed.

Eventually, the trio became separated, and it was while Phoebe was alone in the throng that she suddenly found herself standing beside a very familiar figure. Lady Stainford stood out even amid the tightly packed herd of well-dressed guests, for she had the most vivid hair and the most conspicuous bosom of any woman present. Phoebe, forced by her surroundings into at least a semblance of politeness, decided to address her rival.

"Good evening, Clarissa," she said frostily. "Terrible squeeze, is it not?"

"Why, Phoebe," Clarissa responded, with a look of barely concealed animosity. "I did not expect to find you here. But it seems that all of London is present—from the highest to the lowest."

"That certainly would explain your presence." Phoebe could almost swear that she heard the other's jaw clench!

"I do not see Charles here tonight," Clarissa said presently. "Has he deserted you?"

Phoebe caught her breath sharply at such audacity. Had this woman no shame, no remorse whatsoever? "You know as well as I do why Charles is not with me," she whispered fiercely. "I am sure you must find the whole situation vastly entertaining."

"I beg your pardon?" Clarissa exclaimed, with a look of startled surprise.

"Am I not behaving as you expected?" Phoebe inquired with bitter irony. "Pardon me. I had quite forgotten. A wife is not supposed to display her awareness of her husband's indiscretions, is she?"

For a moment, Clarissa's countenance remained quite blank. Then a slow smile of infinite satisfaction lifted the corners of her full red lips. "I am surprised to see you so upset over so trifling a matter."

Phoebe was sickened by such cool indifference. "Is Charles merely another conquest?" she asked. "Does he mean nothing to you?"

"He obviously means a great deal to you." Clarissa slowly unfurled her painted silk fan, waving it languidly before her. "It is always a mistake to allow a man to become too important in one's life. Men are notoriously fickle, I vow—as you must be well aware."

"Yes," Phoebe admitted, barely suppressing the urge to rake her nails across that lovely face. "I have had experience enough of men's fickleness."

Clarissa's look was pitying now. "Then I suggest that you accept defeat as gracefully as possible and find some other diversion."

"No!" Phoebe said, more forcefully than she had intended. "I stood by once before and let you waltz off with my husband. But not this time. You shall not have Charles!"

"He is a wonderful lover, is he not?" Clarissa purred, her eyes narrowed and gleaming in triumph. "I suppose I should not blame you for being annoyed with me. But can I help it if the men you marry prefer my bed to yours?"

Phoebe felt her temper rising at each wicked word from her opponent. "If it is a fight you wish for, Clarissa, then you shall have it. I will do anything to free Charles from your toils, you heartless, scheming jade!"

"My, my!" Clarissa replied, perfectly self-assured. "How vulgar we are becoming. I never suspected you could be so passionate. But you cannot win. You see, I am quite ruthless when it comes to getting what I want—and keeping it."

Phoebe very nearly stamped her foot in her rage. "This is one man you shall not keep!" she declared. "Charles is mine."

"Well met, fair ladies!" their host hailed them over the din. "I trust you are enjoying my little gathering."

"I vow I have never enjoyed an evening more," Clarissa said with obvious sincerity.

The Duke's plump cheeks puffed with pride, while his tightly laced figure looked as if it might burst the buttons on his form-fitting coat. "And you, my dear Mrs. Hargood?" he asked, turning expectantly toward Phoebe.

"It is a night which I shall never forget, Your Grace," Phoebe acknowledged, summoning the tightest of smiles. Thank God he had intervened before she lost control and gave Clarissa the black eye she so richly deserved. A public brawl would have set the seal on a most disastrous night.

Phoebe soon extricated herself and set out to discover the whereabouts of her two friends. It was some time before she was able to locate them in the crush, and Douglas was quite put out by her request to be taken home. Letty was much more sympathetic.

"I told you not to come tonight," she reminded Phoebe. "I knew it would be too much for you."

"You seemed perfectly well earlier on," Douglas said, a touch of reproach in his voice.

"But I am not well now!" Phoebe snapped. "And unless you wish to see me lying insensible at your feet, you will take me home and not stand there prosing on like a bagpipe."

He patted her shoulder pacifically. "No need to fly up into the boughs, my dear. We are leaving at once"

Phoebe summoned enough courtesy to apologize. "I am sorry to curtail your pleasure, Letty."

"Never mind about that," her friend reassured her. "To own the truth, it was not nearly as entertaining as I had hoped it would be."

"Horribly dull," Douglas agreed before leading them out.

During the carriage drive, Douglas and Letty carried on a low-toned conversation while Phoebe pressed herself into a corner, her eyes closed in an attitude of exhaustion that was not entirely feigned. The recent scene with Clarissa had left her feeling curiously limp, and she did not even rouse herself to bid Letitia goodnight when that damsel alighted at the home of her parents.

Phoebe could not recall her behavior that evening without a shudder. Not that she regretted anything she had said, but she had come perilously close to making a spectacle of herself.

Boasting that she would get Charles out of the clutches of that infernal woman! Brave words, to be sure. But how was she to accomplish this noble design? Nevertheless, it must be done—not only for her own sake, but for Charles's as well.

"You shall not have him, Clarissa!" she muttered to herself. "No, no, no!"

"What?" Douglas exclaimed, his startled cry making Phoebe aware that she had unconsciously spoken her thoughts aloud. "What is it, Phoebe?" he continued, naturally confused.

"I am going home," she stated firmly.

"Well of course you are," he said, looking a little apprehensive now. No doubt he thought she was all about in the head. "We shall be there in a trice."

"Not there!" she cried impatiently. "I am going to Camberley."

Douglas actually blanched at this lunacy. "We cannot possibly go to Camberley tonight," he said. "It is much too far. Are you certain you are quite well?"

"I have no intention of driving all the way to Hampshire tonight," Phoebe replied. "What an idiot you are, Douglas."

He looked most relieved to hear this. "Oh. Well, when the season is over, of course—"

"I do not mean to wait for that either. I shall be leaving in two or three days at most."

Douglas was horrified. "But Phoebe! What of Letty?"

Fingering her chin absently, Phoebe considered this. "She had better come with me."

"If you are taking Letty with you," Douglas said with determination, "then I am coming too. Not that I can conceive why you must be rushing off to the country like this, unless—" he paused, looking at her in some anxiety. "I say, Charles is not ill, is he? I have been wondering why he has not returned to London."

Phoebe decided that it was time she admitted someone into her confidence. Douglas might not be exactly needle-witted, but neither was he a complete clunch. He could be trusted to keep his own counsel. Besides, he was an old and loyal friend. Who else could she turn to, after all?

"Charles has no intention of returning," she said in a toneless voice. "He has made it clear that he wants nothing to do with me."

"What!" Douglas was dumbfounded. "You must be mistaken, Phoebe."

She felt as if her throat was closing up, but it was too late now for reticence. "Perhaps I should inform you that there is someone else involved. Yes," she affirmed in answer to his look of startled inquiry. "Charles has formed a—a connection with Lady Stainford."

After a moment of absolute silence, Douglas burst out laughing. "I might have known you were trying to hoax me. Charles and Lady Stainford! It is too absurd."

"Dash it!" Phoebe cried, angry at his refusal to believe her. "Do you really think I would joke about something like this? They are lovers, I tell you! Why, Clarissa admitted it tonight to my face. How else could she know what a superb lover he is?"

Douglas could hardly be blamed for finding no suitable response to this question, which was entirely rhetorical in any case. One thing, however, had become abundantly clear to him, as his next words revealed. "Phoebe! You are in love with Charles."

"That is beside the point," she insisted, not wishing to admit this all-too-probable explanation for her actions. "Charles is my husband, and I will not share his attentions with Clarissa or any other woman."

"You made no such objection to sharing Robert," Douglas said with a sly glance.

Phoebe glared at him. "If you wish to accompany Letty and me to Camberley, you had better learn to keep your tongue between your teeth."

"Forgive me," he said, taking her hands in his and regarding her with real affection. "It seems that we are both in a similar predicament. Perhaps at Camberley our luck will change." He smiled wryly. "We may even be of some assistance to each other. If there is anything I can do, you need only ask me, my dear."

Phoebe responded at once to the warm sincerity of his tone. She might have known she could rely on Douglas. "Thank you," she said, returning his clasp. "Who knows? I may yet have need of your services."

~/~

Phoebe's threat to depart the city within three days was not an idle one. The following day she managed to coax Letty into leaving the delightful follies of the season—even exaggerating, with delicious mendacity, her slight indisposition.

Then, after a frenzy of activity involving the packing of trunks and bandboxes and the controlling of nervous abigails, they set out for Hampshire in Douglas's own private conveyance.

As the sights, sounds, and smells of London disappeared behind them, Phoebe was conscious of a growing feeling of apprehension about meeting Charles again after such a bitter separation. Letty, at least, seemed quite content to face a period of quiet rustication. Douglas, seated beside her, could not conceal his pleasure. He was in an absolute ecstasy at the thought of having Letty all to himself for a few weeks.

They arrived at Camberley in the cool of the evening, quite unannounced. After the long drive, the sight of the house—a graceful yet solid edifice from the age of Wren— was strangely comforting to Phoebe. She had always loved the spaciousness and understated elegance of Camberley and felt, indeed, that she had come home.

Gathering her courage, she marched boldly into the front hall—there to be stopped short by a most disagreeable sight. Whatever she had expected, it was certainly not this.

Crossing the hall directly before her was a woman whom she had not thought to see in this house for some time to come—if ever. So startling was the sight that Phoebe could not keep from exclaiming, "Good grief. Olivia! What, in heaven's name, are you doing here?"

Chapter Twelve

"Miss Loftbury is here with me, Phoebe," a commanding voice spoke from the doorway to her left. Phoebe turned to confront Charles's sister, Hortense Dunstan, Lady Chilton. It seemed that the house was overrun with disagreeable people!

Before Phoebe could react to this intelligence, Charles himself emerged from directly behind Lady Chilton. When brother and sister stood together as they did now, it was easy to see the resemblance between them. Both were rather stocky in build, with dark hair and eyes and a decided chin. But Charles's eyes held a warmth that his sister's lacked, and his rare smile was surprisingly sweet while hers was no more than a perfunctory twist of the lips.

"My sister and Miss Loftbury are guests here for the next few weeks," Charles said, expanding on Hortense's statement. He was looking rather stern, but that was not unusual for him. It was one of the most disconcerting things about him, Phoebe thought, that she could seldom tell from his features what he might be thinking.

Phoebe experienced a sudden urge to cast herself into his arms. In order to counteract this rather unseemly desire, she launched quickly into speech. "But what a happy coincidence!" Hearing Letty and Douglas as they made their belated entrance behind her, she explained, "I too have brought guests. We shall be quite a gay party, shall we not?"

She was interrupted in the painful procedure of introductions by the arrival of her mother-in-law, who hailed her as the prodigal daughter. "Phoebe!

What a wonderful surprise! I am so glad you are come."

Here, at last, was someone Phoebe could greet with unalloyed pleasure—and she did so, giving Charles's mother a warm hug. "I am very happy to be here again," she said, "but I fear I have only brought you further inconvenience. Two extra guests to accommodate!"

"The inconvenience must be your own," Mrs. Hargood responded with a laugh. "You are mistress here, remember. The dower house is not yet ready for me to move into, but I already consider myself merely a visitor at Camberley. It is your home now, my dear."

Phoebe had almost forgotten this. "Why, so it is," she said in some surprise. "I must see to my guests then. I shall consult with Mrs. Lewis directly. But I hope you will not desert me, Mama. I depend upon you to smooth my path with the servants. I would not wish to offend anyone."

"As to that," Lady Chilton announced majestically, "I believe I can take care of any problems connected with the staff."

"How terribly kind of you, my dear Hortense," Phoebe said sweetly. "But you are also a visitor here, and I do not put guests to work in my home."

Having thus neatly disposed of her sister-in-law, Phoebe excused herself and led Mrs. Hargood away. The next half hour was spent arranging for the comfort of her guests and ingratiating herself with the housekeeper. This last was not difficult, as Mrs. Lewis was already acquainted with her new mistress and had taken a liking to the young woman from the start. Besides which, as Phoebe soon learned, she was fanatically devoted to Charles. Anything Mr. Hargood did could not be wrong, and any wife he chose must be a fine lady, indeed

Everything was soon in train, but before rejoining the others, Phoebe could not resist asking Charles's mother how her son had been.

"As cross as crabs," Mrs. Hargood replied instantly. "One hardly dares speak to him these days. And he is so busy! When he is not locked in his study, he is out supervising the repairs to the dower house."

"If he is working too hard, it is no wonder that he should be disagreeable. He looks a trifle pale."

"He does. But I believe there is more to it than that. Phoebe—" Mrs. Hargood stopped abruptly, as if unsure how to go on. "Phoebe, why have you never written since he returned home? And why did he return alone? Have you quarreled?"

Not knowing how to answer so direct a question, Phoebe bit her lip. "You had best ask Charles," she said at last.

"Oh, I already have," replied the amazing Mrs. Hargood. "He tells me not to worry. But I am worried, Phoebe. I do not like it at all. I am sure that a great deal of his trouble is that he has been missing you."

"One would not guess it from his reception today."

The other woman paid no heed to this pathetic response. "It is merely fatigue, I daresay. That, and the annoyance of having Olivia and Hortense here. I know she is my own daughter," she added briskly, "but Hortense is a confirmed meddler. Charles will not stand for that much longer."

Phoebe patted her shoulder affectionately. "You will not mind, then, if I give Hortense an occasional set-down?"

"Not at all," Mrs. Hargood said with perfect placidity. "It is just what she needs. But," she added, returning as always to the point, "I still think you and Charles should have a nice long talk. It is not good for a married couple to spend so much time apart. Why, at this rate, I shall never live to see my son's children!"

"Charles could have come to me as easily as I have to him," Phoebe answered tartly, disregarding her concluding remark.

Mrs. Hargood sighed. "They never do, my dear. Men are very silly about such things—even the best of them. But," she continued, brightening, "now that you are here, we shall be much more the thing!"

~/~

Charles, however, was not so sanguine. Shut up in his study, he saw little to rejoice at in his wife's presence. Aside from the shock of her sudden appearance—for which he had been completely unprepared—the whole thing had placed him in a most awkward position.

It had been almost seven weeks since he had run away from London. Yes, that was what he had done. He had run home to mother like a sniveling schoolboy. These past weeks had been anything but easy.

His home had always been a refuge, a place of peace and contentment where he had escaped from the world and calmed his spirit in quiet solitude. But for once Camberley refused to work its magic. Its power to soothe had vanished, along with other fond illusions. Without Phoebe, nothing mattered.

More than once he had been on the point of returning to London. He just wanted to be near her again. Surely that would be enough. But he knew it could not be. And when he thought how hateful his presence would be to her, he sank even lower into the depths of despair.

He had ample time for reflection, however. And, as he dwelt more and more on his relations with Phoebe over the years, he understood more clearly than ever how much he had been lying to himself.

He recalled, in amazing detail, the first time he had met the woman his cousin Robert had married after so brief a courtship. Knowing Robert, he had expected that his bride would be beautiful. But nothing had prepared Charles for the emotions he felt when Robert introduced him to Phoebe. She was the most captivating, the most desirable woman he had ever beheld. Clever, too, and full of her own special mischievous spirit.

In short, she was everything a man could possibly wish for. And Charles had never been more of a man than at that moment.

Damn Robert! Charles thought bitterly. Handsome, charming, self-confident Robert. Charles had envied his cousin's way with the ladies before, but never had he come so near to hating him as the day he realized Robert had captured a woman Charles would have given his soul to possess.

Shocked at the violence of his feelings, Charles had immediately begun to confuse them. After all, it was one thing to admire an attractive woman, and quite another to find yourself lusting after your cousin's wife. Consequently, he behaved with greater stiffness than ever and gave all the appearance of a man who considered the lady beneath his touch.

Phoebe, in turn, had done her possible best to provoke him, and succeeded so well that it was not long before he was telling himself that she was nothing but a shallow, silly baggage who deserved the husband she had chosen.

After that, he had done everything in his power to avoid meeting the chit. A well-meaning acquaintance had repeated to him one of Phoebe's witticisms at his expense, and he had responded in kind. Every subsequent meeting between them had merely been a variation or elaboration on that original theme. It was as if they were deliberately building a wall between them—a wall of words, with each equally determined to keep the other safely on the other side. And then, one morning, they found themselves in bed together and, in spite of their best efforts, the wall had crumbled about them. Yet now they were more surely divided than ever.

Charles could no longer pretend to himself that he did not love Phoebe. He had always loved her. But she must never know. She must not suspect that he had committed this last and greatest folly of all.

When he heard Phoebe's voice in the hall earlier, it had been sweeter to him than any chorus of angels. Then he had stepped out to meet her, only to see Douglas Ardshire standing beside her. How could she? After all these weeks, how could she show up here with her latest flirt in tow? The brazenness, the effrontery of it almost defied belief!

Things had been difficult enough with Hortense and Olivia here. Olivia was a born nuisance. A broomstick had more animation, and probably more intelligence. How he could ever have considered marrying her was beyond him. He recalled it with a feeling of nausea and wondered why in God's name Hortense had been fool enough to bring her to Camberley again.

But of the two, he preferred Olivia to his sister, who continually repeated the most scandalous *on-dits* regarding Phoebe's conduct in London since he had left. Her *cicisbeos*, it appeared, were legion—and foremost among them was Lord Douglas Ardshire. Rumor had it that Phoebe and Miss Comston never stirred without him. Olivia merely acted as an echo at these recitals, corroborating every spiteful word spoken by his sister. He was now barely able to feign civility in the presence of either.

And yet, here was Phoebe, apparently bent on

proving the worst of the tales about her to be true. She was full of fun and gig, and Ardshire was smiling like a complete mutton-head. Miss Comston alone, he reflected, looked a little uncomfortable. But she was too much of a pea-goose for that to mean anything.

It would have given Charles the greatest pleasure to plant Lord Douglas a facer. He could, too. But that would certainly be a queer way for a host to greet his guest. So he had taken himself off to his study, where he now sat in solitary state.

Considering and reconsidering the situation, Charles's anger grew in direct proportion to his suspicions. Small wonder, then, that it was a most forbidding-looking gentleman who sat down at the head of the table that night for dinner.

~/~

Phoebe, seated at the opposite end of the table, thought she had never seen her husband looking so grim. He was not happy to see her—that much was certain. But was it really necessary to display his displeasure so openly? Under that basilisk stare, she was sorely tempted to poke out her tongue. But other tactics might serve as well.

Charles's mama was lamenting the shortage of males at table and wishing that dear Lawrence had been with them. Lawrence was Lord Chilton, the unfortunate Viscount whom Hortense had somehow bullied into marrying her. A good twenty years her senior, the kindhearted and courtly gentleman deserved a better partner. He seemed content enough, however, to be under his wife's thumb—especially since she had managed to produce the required heir to ensure the glorious future of the Chilton estate and its attendant titles.

"How does your husband go on, Lady Chilton?" Phoebe asked, looking down the table at her sister-in-law. "His gout does not trouble him, I trust?"

Hortense compressed her lips into a thin, straight line. "My husband is not afflicted with that particular complaint, I am thankful to say."

"I am glad to hear it," Phoebe returned, adding wickedly, "I am sure he has enough on his plate, poor man, without that."

"I do not know what you can mean," Hortense said.

Impaling a slice of capon with her fork, Phoebe paid no attention to this but turned toward Olivia. "And how is your dear mama, Miss Loftbury?" she questioned. "It is an age since we met."

Since Olivia and her mother had successfully avoided any contact with Phoebe in London, this reference could only be to that memorable scene at the door of Charles's bedchamber. Olivia, to Phoebe's great delight, turned as scarlet as an officer's coat. She began to stammer something incoherent but was forestalled by Charles—who must, Phoebe thought, be dreading where this conversation might lead if left in her hands.

"Have you been enjoying the season, Miss Comston?" he inquired, perfectly cool.

But Letty, who, along with everyone else, had been mesmerized by the interchange between Phoebe and Olivia, was unprepared to answer. "I beg your pardon, sir?" she said, blinking at him stupidly.

Charles patiently repeated the question, and this time Letty obliged with an exhaustive description of her experiences in town. Charles might be stuffy and possessed of some antique notions, but Phoebe could not fault his handling of this situation. He had neatly turned the conversation and listened to Letitia's catalogue of trivialities with all the appearance of interest. Even her artless comments on her presentation and the affability of the Prince Regent caused no more than a quiver of his lips.

"What a gay life you have been leading," Charles said in a colorless voice when Letty at last paused for breath. "With so many inducements to remain, I wonder what can have caused you all to quit London before the season was over. I am afraid you will find it very dull here at Camberley."

"To own the truth," Letty began innocently, "we would never have come down at all, had not Phoebe insisted—"

"Actually, I thought Letty was looking rather tired and that a fortnight at Camberley would do wonders for her constitution," Phoebe said. Her tone was light, but the look she bent upon Letty was designed to silence any attempt to deny this patent falsehood.

Charles was also looking at Letitia, with a quizzical gleam in his eye. "And is there no gentleman," he asked, "whose presence in town might have persuaded you to remain?"

Letty appeared puzzled. "What do you mean?"

"What Charles wants to know," Lord Douglas attempted to elucidate, "is whether you have formed a tendre for anyone."

"Well, of course she has!" Mrs. Hargood put in scornfully. "Every young woman falls in love at least once in her first season. It is quite a tradition."

Letty's eyes flashed. "Then congratulate me on being the first to have broken with tradition! I do not know any man worth loving."

"Bravo!" Phoebe cried. "Spoken like a sensible woman. All this fuss about being in love! I am thankful that I have long put such youthful follies behind me. Be guided by me, Letty," she added, pausing to fortify herself with a tiny sip of wine. "Give your hand, by all means, but not your heart.

Flirtations are much more amusing and far less dangerous so long as one is reasonably discreet."

"You speak from experience, I presume," Lady Chilton said with a sneer.

"Of the broadest kind," Phoebe acknowledged—a piece of spite which she could not resist.

Dinner was soon over and the party moved into the drawing room—with the exception of Hortense, who excused herself and retired early. After a minor altercation over whether to play whist or speculation, it was decided to attempt the former. Olivia declined to play at all, and Charles insisted on remaining at her side.

Phoebe watched in growing consternation as Charles devoted himself to Miss Loftbury. He offered her the most comfortable chair and placed a rug over her knees—an unnecessary act of solicitude on such a warm May evening. Then he drew his chair near to hers and they carried on a softly-accented conversation—the picture of domestic companionability.

All this, Phoebe witnessed from the corner of her eye as she and Douglas began to play against Letty and Mrs. Hargood. Several times Douglas had to call her to book for inattention. But Phoebe had quite another game in mind, with Charles as her opponent. If he wished to demonstrate his preference for Olivia's company, he need not expect his wife to ignore a well thrown gauntlet. She would not merely emulate his example; she would improve upon it.

Douglas, she knew, was still smarting from Letty's emphatic assertion that she loved no man. He might welcome this chance to simulate an interest in Phoebe, and thus give Letitia a little food for thought. Besides, he had promised her his assistance. Here was his opportunity.

"Douglas," she said at the first auspicious moment, "I do believe we were made to be partners."

Apparently, Douglas knew her well enough to catch her intention, and he promptly responded in a similar vein. "So I told you," he declared, "on the many occasions when I begged you to marry me."

"Oh, to turn back the clock!" Phoebe said soulfully, raising her voice a fraction. "But I do not know that you would make a suitable husband. Husbands are such dull creatures. You are a much more satisfactory flirt."

They continued this style of banter for the rest of the evening, flirting outrageously and laughing too loudly. Yet they still managed to vanquish their opponents. Mrs. Hargood played well enough, paying little heed to Phoebe's charade. No doubt, she knew her daughter-in-law well enough to be aware that it was all mere nonsense.

Letty, on the other hand seemed to be very annoyed. She looked daggers at her two friends, frequently forgot to follow suit, and was obviously not enjoying herself. Finally, she ended the game by saying that she was overtired from the journey and must go to bed.

Douglas was genuinely concerned about her, but Phoebe was feeling quite pleased with the night's work. How much of their performance had been observed by Charles, she was not certain. He appeared unperturbed, but she suspected that he was not unconscious of what had passed at the card table.

If he was angry, so much the better! She had done no more than he had. Not as much, in fact. First it was Lady Stainford—and now Olivia. For a man whom she had once considered something of a dull dog, he did not lack his share of female companions.

Chapter Thirteen

The next morning, Phoebe felt she could not face anyone. She ordered her maid to bring breakfast to her room—an unprecedented act for her—and when she thought that there was least likelihood of being accosted, she made her way downstairs to speak with Mrs. Lewis once more. In the course of their conversation, Phoebe learned that Charles had ridden over to the squire's home with his mother. Miss Comston and Miss Loftbury were walking by the lake with Lord Douglas. She was unable to ascertain where Hortense might be.

Leaving Mrs. Lewis to carry out her instructions for the day, Phoebe returned upstairs to collect her parasol before venturing outside. This took several minutes, for she could not immediately recollect where she had put the confounded thing. When at last, with Rebecca's help, she found it propped up behind a curtain, she took it up and started back down the stairs.

She had not advanced many steps when she heard someone behind her call her name. Turning, she found herself facing Hortense, a threatening sight in a blue and gray gown buttoned high at the neck. What is the woman up to now? Phoebe wondered as she returned her cool good morning.

"I would like to speak with you a moment, if I may," Hortense said, nodding briefly toward the open door of the library.

"Certainly," Phoebe answered politely. They went into the room together and Hortense closed the door behind them. Eyeing each other warily for a few seconds, each was sizing up the other. Neither was much inclined to sit down.

"There is something you wish to say to me, Hortense?" Phoebe asked at last.

"Would you tell me what you are doing here?"

The insolence of this question was such that at first Phoebe could only blink in astonishment. "I beg your pardon?"

"It is bad enough that you are here at all!" Hortense cried with evangelical fervor. "After your scandalous conduct in London the past few weeks—oh yes," she added at Phoebe's evident surprise. "We are well informed on that subject. I do not know how you dare show your face here. But to bring your—your paramour—"

Outraged, Phoebe took a step toward her. "That is quite enough!" she cried. "You have no right to say such things to me. You would not dare to do so if Charles were here."

This produced no more than a curl of Hortense's lip. "Men are such fools," she conceded. "But even Charles could not fail to discern your behavior last night. I was shocked when Olivia told me how you and Lord Douglas conducted yourselves—and in your own husband's presence too!"

"Miss Loftbury is a useful friend indeed," Phoebe said with heavy irony. "For someone with so little sense, she appears to have a great deal to say."

"I might have known you would take this attitude," Lady Chilton said with a look of contempt. "I never approved of your marriage to my brother."

"What a pity," Phoebe said sweetly, "that it is now too late to do anything about it."

"Do not be too sure of that, my dear Phoebe!"

"What do you mean?"

Lady Chilton gave a most unpleasant smile. "In this day and age," she explained, "it is not impossible for a man to rid himself of an unsuitable wife. Such things happen even in the highest circles."

"You surely cannot mean divorce?" Phoebe asked disdainfully. "I never suspected how vulgar you were, Hortense. But you do not know Charles if you think he would ever countenance such a thing."

"Oh, I think he might be brought to see reason."

Hortense wore such a smug, self-confident look that Phoebe wondered just how much of her parasol Hortense's throat could accommodate. "And on what grounds would this imaginary divorce be obtained?" she asked, dangerously quiet.

"Adultery—" Hortense began, but the hateful word had scarce escaped her lips before Phoebe's open palm connected sharply with her cheek. She was too stunned to do more than stare at the woman she had just accused.

"I will not be spoken to in such terms by anyone—especially in my own house!" Phoebe said, shaking with the force of her anger.

Hortense stood nursing her reddened cheek. "Might I remind you, madam, that I was born in this house!"

"And you are likely to expire here if you are not careful."

"How dare you?" Hortense looked likely to explode. "You have already assaulted me, and now you threaten me with further voilence. Charles shall certainly hear of this! And I hardly think he will approve of his wife behaving like a fishmonger."

Phoebe paid no heed to this. "You may be thankful that I hold your mother and brother in such esteem," she said. "Otherwise, you would never spend another night beneath this roof." She drew herself up stiffly. "And if you ever so much as mention this subject to me again, you will most certainly regret it."

Phoebe did not wait to hear Hortense's response, if, indeed, she was capable of responding, but stalked out of the room and out of the house. She could not get away from that impossible woman quickly enough. Never had Phoebe so completely lost control of her temper. But she had never before been so grossly insulted. In any case, she had merely done what many others had wished to do but had not the courage for. She had slapped her sister-in-law. And, to be perfectly honest, she did not regret it. She felt a thrill of pure, unalloyed satisfaction at the memory.

Was everyone determined to separate her from her husband? And what of Charles? Might her recent conduct actually induce him to accept his sister's suggestion? Would he truly find Olivia a more suitable wife?

At a brisk pace, Phoebe made her way around the house to the garden. A stroll through the park would have been even more efficacious, but she had no desire to meet with Olivia and her companions. One confrontation was enough.

The garden, though not large, was well laid out with pleasant paths. Phoebe soon found the bright colors of the spring flowers in their ordered, well tended beds, were having a soothing effect. The day was a delightful one—not oppressively hot, but just warm enough to be enjoyable.

Presently, she discovered a favorite spot—a shaded corner with a conveniently placed bench, where she sat down to inhale the scent of fresh-blooming roses and listen to the faint chirp of robins nesting in a branch nearby.

Over an hour she sat there, trying to conceive of a plan to get rid of Hortense and Olivia without resorting to murder. She was no nearer to a solution when a slight crunching sound on the gravel path beside her announced the arrival of Letitia.

"Good day, Letty," Phoebe greeted her. "What

brings you out here alone?"

Letty positioned herself on the bench beside her friend. "I am escaping," she said simply. "I really could not endure another moment in Olivia's company."

"And Douglas?" Phoebe asked, looking around for a sign of him.

"He was not so fortunate."

"Do you mean to say that you abandoned him in his hour of need? Well," she said philosophically, "I suppose someone must endure Olivia—aside from her mother, of course."

Letty shook her head in sad resignation. "I know it is uncharitable and unchristian, but I simply cannot bring myself to like Olivia."

"Charles seems to enjoy her company," said Phoebe, ruthlessly pulling a petal from an unfortunate rose. "He spent most of last evening pinned to her side."

"I am sure he was just being polite," Letty said carelessly. "He behaved with far more propriety than you did."

Phoebe gave her a long, considering look. "You mean my flirting with Douglas? That," she explained, "is an old game we play. It means nothing, believe me. But it helps relieve the tedium of a dull evening."

Letty looked down at the grass, never raising her eyes to Phoebe's face. "Perhaps," she ventured hesitantly, "it means more to Lord Douglas than you think."

So that is it! Phoebe thought. Letty might not realize it, but she was obviously far from indifferent to Douglas. In fact, if Phoebe did not misunderstand her demeanor, she was jealous! No wonder the child had acted so strangely last night. If Phoebe had not been so preoccupied with Charles, she would have recognized the signs at once.

An interesting development, indeed—and one

very much in Douglas's favor. She had better encourage it. "I never considered it before," Phoebe said now, gazing at Letty through her long lashes. "It is possible, I suppose..."

Letty's look was mournful but stoic. "I am sure he cares for you."

"As a friend," Phoebe insisted, stifling a growing urge to laugh. Could anything be more absurd?

"His feelings may be deeper than mere friendship," Letty said with some difficulty. "Are you certain that you are not in love with him, Phoebe?"

"Quite," Phoebe answered bluntly. "But I am most perturbed! I did not suspect that I might be inadvertently causing Douglas pain—that he could be nursing a secret passion for me all these years."

Letty's distress at this romantic picture was almost Phoebe's undoing. She hardly knew whether to laugh or to weep. While she did not wish to make anyone unhappy, this was definitely a case where one "must be cruel only to be kind."

"You are very beautiful," Letty suggested, rather grimly it seemed to Phoebe.

"Thank you, my dear," she replied, patting Letty's hand. "But I assure you that I am not at all the sort of woman to make Douglas happy. We should not suit." With the most innocent air in the world, she pressed on earnestly. "He needs a younger, more gentle kind of girl—someone more like yourself."

Letty stared, blushing furiously. "Like m-me?" she asked. "Oh no! I am much too ordinary, not at all the sort to—no! You are teasing me, Phoebe. I am sure you would have made a much better—"

"Enough!" Phoebe stopped her in mid-praise. "I can never see Douglas as anything but a friend. Besides, I am a married woman."

"But—" Letty paused, then seemed to decide that she had better finish what she had begun.

"Forgive me, Phoebe, " she said. "But you have been so strange lately that I made sure your heart was involved—that you were in love with someone."

It was amazing, Phoebe thought, how Letty could be so foolish and so wise at the same time. "And you assumed it must be Douglas?" she asked.

"Then it is true!" Letty cried, correctly interpreting Phoebe's question as an admission. "You <u>are</u> in love! But if not Lord Douglas, then who...?" Here Letty halted, her eyes growing round and she drew in her breath in pure surprise. "Phoebe! You cannot—it cannot be—"

With one brisk movement, Phoebe stood up, opening her parasol. "I think we had better return to the house," she said firmly. "The weather is beginning to turn—and I, for one, do not wish to be rained upon."

Letitia accepted this rebuff without demur. She stood quietly, looking at Phoebe as if she beheld her for the very first time. They began to walk back, but Phoebe felt she must say something to distract her friend's thoughts.

"I have been discussing with Mrs. Lewis the possibility of holding a ball here," she offered.

"Oh Phoebe!" Letty was instantly diverted. "When?"

Phoebe smiled. "I thought a week should be time enough to alert the neighborhood," she replied. "It is not to be a large ball, you know. Twenty families, perhaps—no more."

They continued to discuss the details of the ball until they reached the house—what preparations must be made, what gowns they should wear, and who was to be invited. Phoebe doubted that Letty had forgotten their previous conversation, but at least it had been put aside for the present. As for the interview with Hortense, Phoebe had fully recovered from its effects. Hortense had received no more than was her due. Phoebe only hoped that she would now have the good sense to restrain her propensity to interfere in her brother's life. It was a dangerous pastime at best.

~ / ~

Hortense, however, was not so easily put off. While Phoebe was sitting quietly in the garden, Charles and his mother had returned from the squire's home to be confronted by Hortense—who looked to be in a towering rage. Mrs. Hargood, taking one look at her daughter, beat a hasty retreat, murmuring something about sewing, to which neither of her offspring paid any attention.

"I would like to have a word with you in private, Charles," Hortense said in that horribly toplofty tone of hers, which made even the mildest request sound like a command.

Charles raised an eyebrow slightly, but he accompanied her to his study without comment, merely ushering her in with a curious glance at her furious countenance. What trouble had she been stirring up? he wondered. It seemed he could not leave his home for a moment—at least not when Phoebe was there, for he did not doubt that his wife was in some way responsible for this.

"May I ask, Charles, what you intend to do about Phoebe?" Hortense demanded, immediately confirming his suspicions.

"What do you mean, Hortense?" he returned. "What has Phoebe done now?"

Hortense seated herself stiffly in a comfortable chair. "Surely you are not blind, brother," she said. "Phoebe's conduct toward myself I am willing to overlook—"

"Most gracious of you, I am sure," Charles cut in, an edge to his voice which should have warned his sister. Needless to say, she ignored it.

"But her conduct in general," she continued, "has been so reprehensible that no one can overlook it! Her coming to Camberley at all was most impudent and—"

"You seem to forget, sister," Charles said, his hands gripping the arms of his chair till the knuckles gleamed white, "that this is now Phoebe's home."

This was too much for Hortense. Her face froze into a mask of disgust. "It is insupportable!" she exclaimed. "For that woman to be mistress of Camberley!"

"That woman," Charles replied, his face quite as rigid as his sister's, "happens to be my wife. I would advise you to say no more, Hortense. This is no concern of yours."

They faced each other like tigers, each uncertain as to when the other might spring.

"Do you expect me to sit idly by while my own brother is made a laughing stock?" the lady insisted. "I hope I know my duty to my family better than that!"

"Your sense of duty," said Charles, "is wonderful indeed. Would that your discretion were equally strong."

Totally impervious to sarcasm, Hortense compounded her arguments with fatal clarity. "You should never have married her, Charles!" she declared vehemently. "It was a mistake from the beginning. And it is high time you put an end to this farcical marriage."

"Do I understand you correctly?" he asked, unable to credit his hearing. "Are you suggesting that I divorce my wife?"

She could not bring herself to meet his eyes, but looked him directly in the chin. "I know it is not the most respectable course," she admitted. "But this situation is impossible."

"For whom?" he asked drily.

"I have spoken with Olivia," she said, carefully adjusting the long sleeves of her gown, "and I am fairly certain that she could be persuaded to consent to a reconciliation—once Phoebe is out of the way..."

Charles was sickened by the cool complacency of this vulgar suggestion. "How busy you have been on my behalf," he said icily. "But what makes you think that I would offer for Olivia even if I did agree to this wild scheme of yours?"

"Well, naturally, I assumed—" she began.

"Let me be perfectly frank, my dear Hortense," Charles said, leaning forward the better to emphasize his words. "No man who is worthy of the name would ever wed a hen-witted female like Olivia after having a woman like Phoebe. You may have once persuaded me to consider Olivia acceptable as a wife, but I am not such a jackass as to do so a second time!"

Hortense was somewhat alarmed at the uncompromising tone of this speech but appeared as determined as ever to have things her way. "Olivia, in my opinion, is the most suitable match for you. But there are other females who might do almost as well, if you are so set against her."

Charles's patience was perilously close to vanishing like morning mist, but he managed to control himself sufficiently to respond with creditable composure. "You are wasting your breath. To put it plainly, my dear sister, nothing you could possibly say will ever make me consider divorcing Phoebe. This discussion is now at an end."

The lady unwisely chose that moment to lose her temper. "You must be mad!" she cried. "To allow that creature to cuckold you in your own house—"

Charles rose from his seat with such suddenness that he was standing over Hortense before she was even aware of it. Even she could not mistake the fury in his look, and she actually shrank back as he loomed above her, her words dying away on a raggedly drawn breath.

"I have never in my life struck any woman," Charles said, every syllable taut with suppressed anger, "but if you ever again utter one word against my wife, you will have your ears soundly boxed! I am heartily sick," he concluded bitingly, "of your attempts to come between Phoebe and me."

"I have heard quite enough," Hortense said, recovering her sangfroid. "I need not ask, I suppose, how you can speak so to your own sister! It is obvious to me that you are infatuated with Phoebe and will not listen to reason."

"Just so," he responded, stepping back to allow her to rise. Before she could quit the room, however, he addressed her once more. "You were pleased to refer to Phoebe's arrival with her friends as imprudent." She looked at him but said nothing. "I wonder what you call your own presence here with Miss Loftbury?"

"Olivia is an old friend," she said, reddening.

This explanation did not mollify him. "To bring Olivia here was the height of impertinence, not to say ill-breeding," he said, striking with deadly accuracy at her Achilles heel. "You have placed me in the most damnable position."

"I shall pack at once," Hortense said, mortified. "Miss Loftbury and I will leave in the morning."

Charles folded his arms and regarded her blandly. "Much as the prospect pleases me, it will not serve. Such an occurrence would only give our neighbors further food for gossip."

She still did not meet his eye. "What would you have me do, then?"

"You will remain here for the next fortnight, as planned," he said, going to open the door for her. "In the meantime, I am sure you will do nothing that might upset my wife. I should be sorry to see you leave prematurely."

Hortense retired, a much chastened woman. To be soundly defeated twice in one morning was a humiliation which even Buonaparte had never suffered!

~/~

But Charles, having disposed of her plot so neatly, was in no mood to appreciate the joys of victory. He had defended his wife nobly. But though he might present to his sister a picture of iron resolve and perfect confidence, inwardly he was a man divided.

Though he had never before had reason to doubt Phoebe's basic integrity, her behavior of late had left him shaken. Her flirtation at the card table last night had not gone unnoticed. Ordinarily, he would have dismissed her actions as pure mischief, but he could not deny that their relations at present were not precisely ordinary. Nor could he forget that his own behavior was largely to blame for this.

Guilt and remorse ate away at his very soul. Combined with the seeds of doubt which had been sown by Hortense's repetition of the malicious gossip circulating in London, it was devastating.

Could it be that Ardshire was, indeed, her lover? Douglas had always struck him as being an honorable man, one who would not indulge in sordid affairs. Yesterday, though, he had behaved as badly as Phoebe. And if Douglas had not come here to be near the woman he loved, why had he come? Was this just one of Phoebe's idiotic games, or was it far more serious?

Charles was quite perplexed. There were no less than four people beneath his roof whom he wanted to avoid at all costs. And one of them, God help him, was his wife!

Chapter Fourteen

Phoebe had sent out the invitations to her ball at once. The response was prompt and most gratifying. All the invited guests had accepted, even old Mrs. Clarke, who rarely attended social gatherings. A ball at Camberley, however, was something quite out of the common way. It had been a long time since any event so exciting had enlivened this quiet neighborhood.

For the next few days, life at Camberley settled into a regular, if not very satisfying, pattern. Phoebe was kept busy paying calls on her neighbors and receiving them in return. Everyone was agog to become acquainted with Mrs. Charles Hargood, that fashionable female from London. Some of the older generation were inclined to regard her with misgiving, especially considering the gossip related by Lady Chilton, but the younger set were disposed to like anyone who promised them the noise and nonsense of a ball. Many, of course, already knew her from her occasional visits in the past and only wanted to see whether marriage had changed her, and in what manner.

All who met Phoebe, however, were soon disarmed by her easy manners and undeniable charm. They invariably parted from her with a smile, and the general consensus was that she would do very well.

Despite the favorable impression she was making and the new acquaintances she had formed—some of which promised to be most enjoyable—Phoebe was not happy. Whenever visitors were present, Charles was at her side, the perfect host. If he was not precisely animated on these occasions, at least he was cordial. But as soon as the callers departed, Charles made some excuse for leaving as well. He would retreat to his study, or be about somewhere on the estate, or visiting some friend or other, and Phoebe's only crumb of comfort was the knowledge that he ignored Olivia as much as he did her. More than once, even his mother was moved to apologize for Charles's inattentive behavior.

Phoebe was grateful, at least, that Lady Chilton had not alluded to their confrontation in the library. She was a trifle surprised, however. She would not have thought Hortense the kind of woman to be so easily deterred.

The whole atmosphere at Camberley, Phoebe felt, was strained and excessively uncomfortable. Everyone had something to hide; no one could be at ease. Douglas was still doubtful of Letty's feelings and approached her with caution. Letty herself was determined, it seemed, not to admit that she cared for him. Hortense and Olivia were proving unequal to the task of being polite to anyone but each other. Only Charles's mother was as guileless and unconcerned as ever, but she was much preoccupied with her impending removal and not particularly observant where the others were concerned.

Phoebe was more discouraged than ever. She had come to Camberley in the hope of somehow winning her husband's affection, or at least regaining his respect. But as yet she had hit on no plan whereby this could be achieved. Her hope grew fainter every day.

Charles was more unapproachable than ever and the possibility of healing the breach between them seemed remote. If anything, her presence only seemed to make things worse. And flirting with Douglas, she had to admit, was not the wisest thing she had ever done.

She desperately needed someone—some female—to talk with. But who? Letty was too young, and Charles's mother was a dear soul, but too closely involved. To whom could she turn for counsel?

In the end, a confidante was provided from a rather unexpected quarter. Phoebe had promised to pay a visit to Stephen Dodd and his wife, and when at last she fulfilled her promise, she found Emily Dodd alone.

Emily, a short, plump woman with curling brown hair and a cherubic smile, shared her husband's good-humored nature, combined with a warm heart and a good deal of quiet common sense. Though Phoebe had met her only twice before, it would have seemed silly for either of them to use any other than their Christian names.

Emily began by apologizing for Stephen's absence. "He will be very disappointed to have missed you. You and Charles are great favorites with him—and with me too, I assure you."

"It is kind of you to say so, Emily," Phoebe answered politely.

"Fustian!" Emily said with a smile. "It is fact, my dear—not flattery. But I am surprised to see you alone. You are quite welcome," she added earnestly, "to bring your guests along, you know."

Phoebe gave a little grimace. "To own the truth, I am all too grateful for this opportunity to escape my guests for an hour or two."

"Is it as bad as that?" Emily asked with ready sympathy.

"I do not wish to sound churlish," Phoebe said. "But I cannot pretend that I shall miss Lady Chilton when she goes."

"I quite understand," Emily said with a speaking glance. "Most people only tolerate

Hortense because of Charles and his mother—not to mention her rank!"

"There is certainly no need to mention that!"

"Not as long as Hortense has a tongue in her mouth," Emily agreed, bringing a smile to Phoebe's lips.

The tea tray arrived at that moment, and while Emily poured they began to discuss the upcoming ball.

"I hope you will enjoy it," Phoebe said.

"There can be no doubt of that, my dear! Why, the entire neighborhood is positively humming with your ball. No one can talk of anything else."

Phoebe selected a sweetmeat from the small dish offered to her. "I fear everyone will be disappointed."

"You underestimate yourself, Phoebe." Emily directed a penetrating look at her. "But I am concerned that you do not overtax yourself. You do not think you may have undertaken too much at this time?"

Phoebe very nearly jumped at this question. Surely Emily could not have guessed? "I am a trifle—tired, Emily," she confessed slowly. "However, I am quite equal to the exertion of a country ball."

"I do not doubt that you are tired." Emily's voice was mild but determined. "But I believe there is more to this than you are telling me. If there is something that troubles you, Phoebe," she went on gravely, "I hope you know that I can be trusted to hold my tongue."

"What do you mean?"

"Forgive me, my dear," Emily began a little diffidently, "but it is clear that things are not as they should be between you and Charles." Phoebe could only stare dumbfounded as Emily continued. "Stephen and I were most concerned when Charles came to be at Camberley alone all these weeks, while you remained in London. Charles, of course, will say nothing. But if there is anything at all that I can do, I wish you will let me help you."

What Phoebe did next amazed her quite as much as it did her hostess. All the pent-up emotions of the past weeks rushed upon her suddenly. "Oh Emily!" she cried, burying her face in her hands. "I am so unhappy—so ashamed!"

Emily came immediately to sit beside her, putting one arm around her shoulders. "There, there, Phoebe," she murmured soothingly. "Surely it cannot be so terrible as that."

"Oh, but it is!" Phoebe wailed. "Do you know what it is like," she asked desperately, looking up at her friend, "to desire a man so much that nothing else matters? To think of him every waking moment? To lie sleepless each night, wanting him beside you?"

That she had shocked Emily was painfully obvious. "I am sorry," Phoebe said, already regretting her uncharacteristic outburst. Jerkily, she stood.

Emily still sat, looking blankly up at her. When she at last spoke, it was with some difficulty. "I had no idea," she said. "Indeed, Hortense told us of your involvement with Lord Ardshire, but I paid little attention to her gossip. I certainly never suspected anything like this!"

Phoebe was confused. "Douglas!" she exclaimed, eyeing Emily in complete surprise. "What has he to do with anything?"

"But was it not Douglas of whom you were just speaking?"

"Douglas?" Phoebe cried again, as if the very name were an insult. "How could you think such a thing, Emily? I was speaking of *Charles*!"

It was now Emily's turn to be confused. "Then Ardshire is not your lover?" she asked, putting one hand up to her forehead.

"Certainly not!" Phoebe was justly angered at such a charge.

"Do you mean to say," Emily demanded, "that this whole faradiddle is all because you have discovered that you have a *tendre* for your own husband?"

"It is more than that," Phoebe declared with conviction. "This is no ordinary passion. This is—this is *lust*!"

Such a confession was too much for Mrs. Dodd's gravity. To Phoebe's utter mortification, Emily threw back her head and laughed until the tears flowed down her plump cheeks. Once she tried to say something but was incapable of speech. Finally she lay back in her chair, exhausted.

"I am glad," Phoebe said stiffly, "to have provided you with so much amusement.

Emily held out a hand. "Pray do not be angry with me," she pleaded. "But there is really nothing wrong with a woman desiring her husband, you know. Your own Bible will tell you as much. My dear father—bless him—was the vicar here," she said, a twinkle in her eye. "I remember him saying that God has nothing against pleasure. He created it!"

"But I have never felt like this before," Phoebe protested.

Emily gave her a curious look. "Not even with Robert?" she asked. "We are neither of us schoolgirls, so I may as well be frank. Was not Robert celebrated for his—his amorous abilities?"

Phoebe shook her head somewhat ruefully. "I cannot speak for other women," she said. "But for me, comparing Robert to Charles is like—oh, like comparing punting on the Thames to crossing the Atlantic. The first is a pleasant excursion. The second is the discovery of a New World."

Emily's brows rose at this fanciful description.

"And does Charles know how you feel?"

"I hope not!"

"Good Lord! Why?" Emily was apparently under the impression that Phoebe had all the intelligence of a plum pudding. Perhaps it was impossible to expect someone else to understand her feelings when she was so uncertain of them herself. But then, Emily did not yet know the whole story.

So Phoebe explained about Clarissa. Emily listened attentively, even interjecting a pertinent question or two. When Phoebe concluded her rather disjointed narrative, Emily remained silent for some time.

"The more I consider the matter," Emily said eventually, her brows drawn together in concentration, "the more convinced I am that you are mistaken. I am not acquainted with Lady Stainford—I know her only by reputation—but she does not sound like the kind of woman to attract Charles."

"How I wish I could believe that!" Phoebe cried fervently.

"I know Charles," Emily insisted. "He is basically very shy and reserved, lacking in confidence where women are concerned. Besides, he does not like redheads."

Phoebe found this incredible. Charles doubting his power to satisfy a woman? It was too fantastic. "What other possible explanation can there be for his behavior?"

Emily gave a wry grin. "I do not know," she confessed. "But only think how near I came to believing that you were in love with Douglas Ardshire. It is fatally easy to misread a person's words and actions."

Phoebe could find little comfort in this. "Even if Charles does not love Clarissa," she said dolefully, "there is no reason to suppose that he cares for me. The truth is, he has always despised me."

"No more than you professed to despise him, as I recall."

"Did I?" Phoebe asked, her eyes on Emily but her mind far away. The way she now felt about Charles seemed so natural, so right. Had there really been a time when her feelings had been different?

Emily's voice intruded upon her musings. "I do not usually like to give advice, Phoebe," she was saying quietly. "But if I were you, I would have a talk with Charles before this situation becomes any more confused. I never said so before, but I am convinced that you and Charles are ideally suited."

"Do you truly believe that?"

"I do." Emily nodded. "And I think it would be a great pity if your marriage should be unhappy because neither of you will be open and honest about your feelings."

~/~

In the event, Phoebe had her *tête-à-tête* with Charles sooner than she had anticipated. Having said good-bye to Emily, Phoebe returned to Camberley at precisely the moment that Charles rode up to the front door on his high-spirited russet-hued blood-horse, Apollo.

Having been out on the estate all day, Charles greet-ed his wife and apologized for his disheveled appearance. Actually, Phoebe thought he looked most attractive with his hair tousled by the wind and his face rather tanned from being out in the sun. Watching him dismount and hand Apollo to the young stable hand, she wondered uneasily how she herself looked. Fagged to death, probably—if her feelings were any indication.

"Charles," she said hesitantly, as they entered

the house together, "may I have a word with you?"

"Now?" he asked, frowning.

"If it is not too inconvenient."

His look was not encouraging. But despite the fact that he obviously thought it very inconvenient, he consented and led her to his study. Phoebe seated herself with great care while Charles took a chair facing her. He seemed to have developed an inordinate interest in the toes of his riding boots, for his gaze remained fixed on them while Phoebe fidgeted in her seat, wondering how to open this conversation.

"We cannot go on like this, Charles!" she said at last, her voice harsher than she had intended.

At least it effectively claimed his attention, for he looked up at once. "Like what?" he asked, equally harsh.

This was worse than Phoebe had feared. It was apparent that he had no intention of making this easy for her. "Our—our marriage," she began awkwardly, seeking in vain for a delicate approach. "It is impossible!"

Charles's control snapped with terrible suddenness. "Impossible!" he cried, not rising but leaning threateningly toward her. "No doubt that is why you brought your lover here—into my own home."

"What!" Phoebe almost shouted in astonishment. Did everyone believe Douglas to be her lover?

"You are right, madam," Charles continued, his voice as cold as his eyes were fiery. "It is an impossible situation, entirely of your own making. I was a fool to think that marriage to you would be anything but misery."

Phoebe's temper rose with every word, until her wrath quite matched his own. "No doubt you think Olivia would be a much more suitable wife!" she shot back, her eyes ablaze.

"At least," he returned, "she would show more respect for me than you have done!"

Phoebe would hear no more. Trembling with anger, she stood to face her accuser. "You abominable hypocrite!" she stormed. "Why do you not admit that your only reason for considering Olivia is because you know she is too insipid to object to your liaison with Clarissa."

Charles leapt to his feet. "What, in the name of all that's holy, are you talking about?"

"Yes!" she said with bitter satisfaction. "You thought I was too stupid to suspect the truth, did you not?"

"What is this nonsense?" he asked. "By God, if you mean to make me the scapegoat in this—"

"Don't lie to me, Charles!" she said, raising a hand as though to hold back his speech. "I have known about Clarissa for some time. She told me herself that you were lovers. Did you think," she added scornfully, "I did not guess the real reason you left town?"

Charles reached out to grab her wrist, gripping it with bone-crushing pressure. "Listen to me, Phoebe," he said roughly. "Lady Stainford means nothing to me. Oh, she was eager enough to get me into her bed." He acknowledged her look of disbelief. "I do not know what she told you, but she was far from pleased when I informed her that the *only* woman I wanted was you."

"Me!" Phoebe gasped out the incredulous monosyllable.

"You must know how I feel about you, Phoebe," Charles said, forcing the words out painfully. "How could you not, after that last night in town?"

Phoebe could not believe her own ears. "Then why did you go, Charles?" she asked. "Why did you leave me?"

His voice was hoarse, his brow wet with sweat

at the tremendous effort of will he was exerting. "Do you not understand, woman? I knew how you must hate me for what I had done—what I had forced you to do—" his grip tightened unmercifully. "I could no longer trust myself with you. Even now, at this very moment, all I want to do is—oh God, Phoebe!"

Before Phoebe could even think of a response to this impassioned speech, she found herself crushed in Charles's arms while his mouth rained kisses of fire over her face and throat. Then his lips sought hers with such intense hunger that it was impossible to deny the truth any longer.

Charles wanted her! All these long weeks of misery had been for nothing. He had wanted her all along, and yet he had let her suffer—had let her believe that he was indifferent, even unfaithful. Of all the cruel, insensate creatures in the world—

She wrenched herself forcibly from his embrace, gasping for the breath his kisses had stolen. "How could you, Charles!" she cried, incensed.

Charles stepped back quickly, as if she had physically struck him. "Forgive me, Phoebe," he said in a stilted, unnaturally humble tone. "It was unpardonable of me. I swear to you I will never again—"

There was a light knock at the study door before it opened and Mrs. Hargood's face peered around it. "I am sorry to intrude, Charles," she said, gently contrite. "But you did promise to meet with Walter Jenkins, the carpenter. He is waiting in the hall."

"Show him in, Mama," Charles replied, keeping his gaze resolutely turned from his wife. "Phoebe and I are finished."

~/~

At that moment, Phoebe wished Charles's

mother at Jericho. Mrs. Hargood could not have chosen a more unlucky moment to interrupt.

Phoebe was horribly aware that she had made a complete bumble-broth of the situation. Her wretched temper! Just when she had been given the chance to set things right between herself and Charles, she had made matters even worse and pushed him farther away instead.

The hurt, the hopelessness in Charles's face as he had dismissed her was the most bitter punishment he could have inflicted. She had only herself to blame if he never came near her again. But she could not allow that. She must find some way to speak with him again. She could not let him go on believing that he had been rejected.

Hurrying upstairs, she sought in her mind for some sign which might help her to plan her campaign. At first it seemed to her impossible that Charles should be unaware of the passion he had aroused in her. Then she recalled Emily saying that he was shy and lacked confidence with women.

No one had ever accused Charles of being in the petticoat line, and if he had any dealings with paphians or other bits of muslin, he had managed to keep them very discreet. Phoebe herself had often dismissed him as being a little too bumpkinish. She cast her thoughts back to the very first time she had met Charles Hargood, at a London party he had been attending with his mama. The whole meeting was still quite vivid to her mind's eye.

This cousin of Robert's had certainly not impressed her with his looks. He was not unattractive, but there were not many men whose features could bear comparison with Robert's classical good looks. Yet there had been something about Charles …

She had felt instinctively that Charles was a

man a woman could rely on, a man who would be faithful and kind, a man who was strong and honorable. In short, he was a man. And she was married to a spoilt, willful child. In all but the most superficial qualities, Charles Hargood was superior. He would make some lucky girl a fine husband. For a moment, she actually hated Charles—hated him because he was free and she was not.

But the look Mr. Hargood had bent upon her on that occasion plainly showed that he thought his cousin's new wife quite beneath his touch. She had been more hurt by the gentleman's cold, hard glances than she cared to admit. She was never one to take insults lying down, however, and she soon detected a number of flaws in Charles's countenance and character which she exaggerated with such comic skill that she had all her acquaintances laughing at the boorish rustic.

Over the years, she and Charles had made the most of every opportunity to pester and plague each other—and there were many. She had soon forgotten—or rather, deliberately suppressed—her first betraying impression of him. But she wondered now at the motives behind much of her behavior.

When any female had shown the slightest interest in Charles, Phoebe soon convinced her that she must have windmills in her head to admire so doltish a man. When she had learned of his engagement to Miss Loftbury, she had been shocked and not particularly pleased.

But neither that nor the unusual tenacity of her contempt had led her to question her feelings for him. Not until his mother's foolish mistake had catapulted them into this fantastic situation, had the carefully constructed edifice of her studied distaste begun to crack. Now that it had collapsed about her, she was amazed that it had stood for so long on such feeble foundations.

But of course it had all been absolutely necessary. While Robert was alive, to have admitted her true feelings for Charles—even to herself—would have been unthinkable. She would never have dishonored her marriage vow, however much it might have cost her to remain faithful. So she had closed her mind and heart to the man she had recognized almost at once as her ideal partner.

Charles's callous attitude toward her had made it easier, of course. By the time Robert died, Phoebe had convinced herself that Charles Hargood meant nothing to her. The thought of marrying him never entered her head. And she was sure he felt just the same.

But now she was his wife. She would soon be the mother of his child. The green girl who had married Robert was now a woman grown. She had found the right man this time and she was not going to lose him!

She was aware of how dreadfully she must have wounded his pride today. She understood all too well how vulnerable he was, if he truly cared for her. Yet how could he be so blind to his own worth? Could he not see how wonderful he was to her? Incredible as it seemed, he believed she despised him! How could she convince him otherwise?

This question continued to plague Phoebe for the rest of the evening. Dinner was an ordeal of unparalleled proportions. Hortense and Olivia sat like two icons in a medieval cathedral. Douglas and Letty were both nervous and on edge. Charles, at the head of the table, vouchsafed an occasional reluctant grunt if addressed directly, but mostly sat in blue-deviled silence.

Mrs. Hargood attempted to assist her daughter-in-law in maintaining polite conversation, but the atmosphere in the room was such that even she subsided eventually into a distressed muteness.

Immediately after dinner, Charles excused himself, saying that he wanted to inspect the work done at the dower house today before retiring.

Phoebe recognized her opportunity at once. She could hardly beg to accompany him, but she could follow him.

And what then? Charles would do nothing to risk another rebuff, so it was up to her. She must seduce him, she supposed. But how did one go about seduction? It would have been easy for a woman like Clarissa, but Phoebe had never done such a thing in her life. She hoped that it would not be difficult, for do it she must.

As soon as Phoebe thought she had given Charles a reasonable head start, she bid her guests good night, claiming that she needed a good rest before the ball tomorrow. And then it was all she could do to dissuade Letty from coming up with her!

Parting from the others, she turned left in the hallway and hurried away—not toward the stairs but the front door. Her woolen shawl drawn tightly about her shoulders, she prayed that she might not have waited too long, that she might not miss Charles in the darkness of the park.

~/~

It took Charles more than a quarter of an hour to walk the circuitous path between Camberley and the dower house. The building would be ready for his mother's removal within the week. The work was almost finished, but that was not the reason he had gone there tonight. He was running away again, as he had from London. Never had his spirit been so oppressed, never had his loneliness been so palpable.

A stray cloud dashed across the moon, obscuring the white gravel before him. The wind had risen since sunset. There would probably be rain later. If he did not hurry, he might have to spend the night at the cottage. Not that it mattered—he did not suppose that he would sleep any better tonight than he had in the past few months.

The pale walls and dark green shutters of the cottage came into view. He went in quickly, bolting the door behind him.

After lighting the small lamp on a nearby table, he moved into the front parlor, where he sat in the semidarkness, contemplating his bleak and most unsatisfactory future—a future in which Phoebe wanted no part. She had made that plain enough today.

He looked out through the window at the murky shadows beyond. Dear God! He was going mad! He could have sworn that he saw Phoebe's face peering in through the window pane. Would her image haunt him forever?

But surely no imaginary wife wore such a look of annoyance nor raised a delicate fist to tap loudly on the glass. It really was Phoebe standing outside! He wondered if he had not, indeed, fallen asleep in the chair and was merely dreaming this. Still, he went to the window and opened the casement.

"For heaven's sake, Charles!" she said at once. "Why did you lock the door? Did you expect housebreakers?"

"What are you doing here?" he asked, bewildered by her unexpected arrival.

"Never mind that," she said, reaching out her hand to him through the opening. "Just help me to climb over the sill."

"Do not be foolish, Phoebe," he protested. "Go around to the door and I will open it."

"Do not put yourself to the trouble," she said, grasping his wrist with one hand and his shoulder with the other. Automatically, he put one arm around her as she stepped over the low sill.

In another few seconds she was inside the room—and in his arms. He put her swiftly from him and retreated to the other side of the parlor, from which safe distance he once more assessed her as she closed the sash and fastened it. "You have yet to answer my question," he said sternly. "Why did you come here tonight?"

An enigmatic smile curved her lips. "I should have thought that to be obvious. I followed you here to talk to *you*."

"Surely you could have waited until tomorrow."

"Actually," she admitted, ignoring his suspicious glance, "I wanted to apologize for my behavior this afternoon—and to explain. Though I think," she added thoughtfully, "that any explanations can wait until after—"

"After what?" Charles was growing more confused with every moment.

Her eyes opened very wide at this, as though she was surprised at his lack of comprehension. "Why, until after you have made love to me, of course!" she declared, and when Charles failed to respond, continued in a tone of quiet long-suffering, "You surely are not going to be difficult about this, Charles?"

Now Charles knew what was happening. He had gone mad—stark, raving mad! All these weeks of frustrated desire, all the doubts and suspicions, had been too much. The agony of her rejection today had proven to be the last straw. He had lost his mind.

"You do not—" he stammered foolishly. "I cannot–"

Phoebe continued to speak in that unnaturally calm manner, and every sentence was more fantastic than the one before. "The last time, " she said, "you insisted that I fulfill my duty as a wife.

Now it is only fair that you should fulfill your duty as my husband." She sounded like a governess lecturing a recalcitrant pupil. "You may as well resign yourself to making love to me, Charles, for I shall not leave this house until you do."

All the time she was speaking, she was moving slowly closer. Now she stood directly before him, her eyes—almost emerald in the lamplight—glowing with…no, it could not be! "You do not mean it, Phoebe," he said sadly. "You do not want me." Her smile was extraordinarily tender. "I hesitate to contradict you, my love, but you are quite mistaken."

Her nearness, the look in her eyes, were making Charles a little giddy. He must hold on to his sanity. This was simply not happening. "After a lover like Robert," he insisted, "you could not possibly want me."

Apparently he had said the wrong thing. Phoebe's eyes blazed, and she stamped one little foot sharply on the floor. "I wish that everyone would stop telling me what a great lover Robert was!" she complained. "The truth is, Charles, that I had more pleasure in one night with you than I had in over three years of marriage to Robert."

The gates of paradise were opening for Charles Hargood, but even so near the threshold, still he hesitated. "What—what are you saying, Phoebe?" he asked, scarcely daring to hope that the impossible might, after all, be true.

"Charles, you idiot!" she cried. "I am trying to tell you that I love you! Now will you make love to me?"

Charles hesitated no longer. "Yes!" he said, pulling her to him with one swift, decisive movement. "I most certainly shall."

Then she was in his arms once more, as he had dreamed a thousand times since London. Only this time he was left in no doubt that his wife was as eager for his attentions as even he could wish. She returned his ardent caresses with a fevered urgency that raised his passion to an almost unbearable pitch. He was not sure which of them was most deranged. All he knew was that, mad or not, he intended to enjoy every minute of this.

"The bed—" she whispered once. "Should we not–"

"But he could not wait. "Phoebe," he groaned, "I want you here—now!"

She pressed herself against him, and he realized with amazement that she was reveling shamelessly in the feel of his body—and her newfound power over it. "Then you shall have me now," she promised with a husky laugh. "And I shall have you, my dearest Charles."

Then there was no more room for words as they slowly sank together onto the fresh new carpet. He knelt above her for a moment, savoring the sight of the incomparable beauty he was about to possess. But she was impatient for her lover to claim her and reached up to pull him down into her waiting arms.

As they came together, the first flash of lightning proclaimed the arrival of the storm outside. But it was a long time before Charles became aware of it. Phoebe was his only reality. Phoebe was his world. Phoebe was his!

Later, as they lay together listening to the raindrops dancing wildly on the windowpanes, Charles asked softly, "How do you feel?"

Her eyes were filled with a wondrous glow. "I feel loved, Charles," she said simply. "I feel so loved."

"You are loved," he answered, his lips against her brow, his right hand tangled in her long dark hair. "More than you can know."

They talked for a long time. There was so much to explain, so much to discover. Each was surprised to find how long they had been beloved. Charles gave a detailed account of his encounter with Clarissa, and Phoebe confessed her deliberate attempt to anger Charles by flirting with Douglas. She also told him the direction of that gentleman's real affections, but he had already lost interest.

"I think I fell in love with you that morning at Camberley when you first kissed me," Phoebe said, tracing his mouth with one soft finger. "It is as well you never did so when Robert was alive."

"I would never have done anything so improper," Charles protested.

This priggish remark was very much the old Charles, and Phoebe could not help laughing. "My love," she declared, "you are absolutely priceless! Here you are, practically naked on the floor, having just made love to me—and still preaching propriety."

Charles smiled somewhat ruefully at her quizzing and caught her finger playfully between his teeth before he replied with mock sternness, "You are a baggage, Phoebe!"

"And you adore me," she added complacently.

"I cannot deny it."

"Did you ever contemplate divorcing me to marry Olivia?" she asked suddenly.

"Not for an instant," he said. "But I did contemplate murdering my sister."

She looked at him with a familiar gleam of mischief in her eye. "I do not think I would really grudge Olivia being your wife—"

"Phoebe!"

"So long," she went on, "as I were your mistress."

He arched an expressive eyebrow. "Would that be enough for you, do you think?"

"Well," she said with disarming candor, "I would much rather be your secret vice than your public duty."

“You are an irresistible vice,” he said against her throat. “And one I intend to indulge in frequently! Do you mind?”

“Not at all,” she said, appearing to give the matter serious consideration. “In fact, the more often, the better.”

He said nothing to this, but stood up slowly, lifting her in his arms as he did so.

“Where are we going?” Phoebe asked, wrapping her arms around his neck.

He strode purposefully toward the parlor door. “Upstairs,” he said firmly. “This time I think we should use the bed.”

Phoebe could only stare. “You do not mean—? But it is too soon! You cannot possibly—”

“Of course I can!” he grinned, ascending the stairs. “Do you doubt me?”

“Prove it!” she commanded. And he did—much to her satisfaction.

Chapter Fifteen

In the morning Phoebe awoke to a strange room, a strange bed, and a reassuringly familiar companion. Charles was sitting on the bed beside her, dressed in his clothing of the previous evening. Phoebe smiled sleepily up at him as he reached out to tenderly brush back a stray curl of dark hair from her brow.

"It is past ten o'clock, my love," he said.

"What does that signify?" she asked, not particularly concerned about time.

"You see," he said, looking at her expectantly, "we have not been home since last night."

Phoebe sat bolt upright in bed, eyeing him in horrified comprehension. She was wide awake now.

"I have taken the liberty," Charles told her, "of fetching your clothes from the parlor. I shall go downstairs while you dress."

Phoebe's brows rose. "It is a little late for modesty now, my dear Charles."

"True," he agreed rather regretfully. "But if I stay to watch, you may never get that damned gown on—and we shall be here all day."

He left the room hurriedly, but Phoebe stretched like a satisfied cat before getting out of bed. It took some time to struggle with her gown unaided. No matter how she twisted and pressed its folds, there was no way to hide its very crumpled appearance—the natural result of its having lain in a discarded heap most of the night. It was a lovely gown, she thought as she eyed the pomona-green silk in the mirror, but hardly appropriate for morning wear.

As for her hair, it was hopeless. Last night it had been charmingly arranged by the indispensable Rebecca in a lovely Grecian style. Now it was down around her shoulders and, try as she might, Phoebe could do nothing with it.

Sighing gustily, she turned and trudged down the stairs. The parlor looked quite chaste and prim in the morning sunlight—hardly a fitting setting for passionate encounters.

"I am a positive scarecrow," she wailed, joining Charles beside the window. "Just look at my hair!"

"Your hair is beautiful," he responded. "And so are you."

The compliment was pleasing but quite misplaced. "Only a man," Phoebe said with a shudder, "would say something so idiotic. Can you imagine," she continued, "what Hortense would say if she saw me like this?"

"You must explain to her," he said solemnly, "that it is the latest fashion—the *dernier cri*—in London."

"*En deshabille*?" she asked, not at all fooled by his resolutely sober countenance. "I would think even less of her if she swallowed that plumper."

"Let us hope that she is not at home, then."

Phoebe closed her eyes at the thought of her sister-in-law's reaction to such a sight. "Is there any way we can slip into the house unobserved?" she asked hopefully. "Some secret entrance, perhaps?"

"I'm afraid," Charles said, chuckling, "that Camberley boasts no such convenience. Besides," he added, "I see no reason why we should sneak into our own home like a pair of thieves."

And so it was that twenty minutes later, at half past eleven in the morning, Mr. and Mrs. Charles

Hargood walked arm-in-arm up to the front door of their residence. They had as fine an audience for their grand entrance as anyone could have wished for.

Simpson, opening the door to them, stared in open-mouthed wonder at the much crumpled couple. But his astonishment was quite eclipsed by the gasp of horror behind him which escaped from the lips of Lady Chilton. She and her mother were standing in the hall with Stephen Dodd, who had arrived just moments before. The squire's eyes twinkled as he bid his friends a bland good morning and was answered in kind.

"What on earth—" Hortense began, but was forestalled by her brother.

"You must excuse us for a few minutes, Stephen, " Charles said with perfect aplomb. "I am sure you will appreciate that Phoebe and I need to freshen up a little. We shall be down directly." He nodded in his mother's direction. "Mama and Hortense will take good care of you, I know."

Charles turned calmly and escorted his wife upstairs—although Phoebe marred their performance somewhat by succumbing, halfway up, to an unseemly fit of giggles that must have been perfectly audible to those below. The last voice they heard as they reached the upper landing was Mrs. Hargood's, happily chirping, "We must grow accustomed to their little oddities, I suppose!"

~/~

Charles returned to his friend before Phoebe was able to complete the more extensive preparations required by a female. Only Mrs. Hargood had remained with their guest, and she soon deserted them with the excuse that she had other duties which could no longer wait.

Facing the knowing look in Stephen's eye,

Charles fumbled a little with his cravat. "I hope you will forgive your rather unorthodox reception, Stephen," he apologized again.

"I quite enjoyed it," the squire said, quizzing him unmercifully. "You and Phoebe seem intent on providing the neighborhood with an unlimited supply of scandal-broth."

Charles frowned slightly. "I hope that this morning's incident will not go beyond these walls."

"With Hortense here?" Stephen asked skeptically, apparently under no illusions as to Lady Chilton's feelings toward Phoebe. "At any rate, it would seem that you and Phoebe have at last settled your differences."

"Yes."

Stephen was not put off by this damping monosyllable. He leaned back in his chair, directing a curious glance at Charles. "I was quite worried," he said, "when you returned home without your wife—who seemed in no hurry to join you!"

Charles exchanged his friend's gaze with a similar one. "You knew I was in love with her, did you not?"

"My dear fellow, I've known that any time these past five years!" Stephen responded, with real amusement.

"How could you?" Charles shook his head, mystified by Stephen's omniscience. "I did not know it myself."

"I was well aware of that also," Stephen answered, then condescended to explain further. "You and Phoebe have always been so aware of each other. I daresay you never noticed how often you mentioned her name in conversation, or how you knew every trick of speech—every expression of hers. And the few times I spoke with her," he added, "she seemed just as bad. She was hardly complimentary, but she could not stop talking about you."

"Yet you never said anything to me?" Charles asked, perhaps justifiably annoyed.

"It would have done no good," Stephen contended. "You needed to discover it for yourselves. I was sure you would, when the time was right. It was not for me to play God."

Charles could only stare at his calm assurance. "Do you realize that, had it not been for my mother's blunder in putting Phoebe in my bedchamber," he said severely, "we might never have discovered it?"

Stephen shrugged. "I am convinced that something would have happened to throw you together. There is no such thing as chance, my boy—whatever some philosophers may say."

"Good morning, Charles—good morning squire," Douglas's voice intruded upon their philosophical speculation. They greeted the newcomer and Charles bade him join them.

Stephen, however, rose to take his leave. He had only come, he said, to see how Phoebe was doing. Having missed her call the previous day, he had been dismayed to learn from Emily that Phoebe was not feeling quite the thing.

"Now I see that is no longer the case, I shall return home. But of course," he added, smiling broadly, "I shall see you all tonight at the ball."

Charles gave a start of surprise. "Good— I had quite forgotten the ball!"

"No doubt you had more important matters to command your attention," Stephen said, and before Charles could respond to this base provocation, he bade them farewell and was out the door.

The squire was hardly out of earshot when Lord Douglas began a somewhat disjointed apology. He wanted, he said, to explain his curious attentions to Charles's wife the last few days, and begged that Charles would hear him out. Having already heard the tale from Phoebe's lips, Charles cut short what promised to be an orgy of remorse.

"Phoebe has already acquainted me with the truth, my dear Ardshire," he said. "It seems I was correct in assuming you had come here in pursuit of a female. I merely mistook your quarry."

"It is very good of you to be so forgiving," Douglas confessed. "I am sensible that my behavior has been reprehensible."

"I have no doubt that you were shamefully coerced. Phoebe can be most persuasive." Charles smiled crookedly. "You may be thankful that I have such excellent self-control. More than once this week I have been within an ace of drawing your cork."

Douglas laughed outright, obviously much relieved to have sorted this out so amicably. "I am indeed grateful," he replied. "All the more so, as you are known to possess a punishing right!"

The talk then flowed naturally into a discussion on prizefighting, correct science, and the merits of various pugilists. At last, Charles excused himself, regretting that he had work yet to do. But before quitting the room, he looked keenly at Douglas, hesitating only the briefest moment. "I think you had best waste no time in offering for Miss Comston," he said.

Douglas was startled by the unsolicited advice but not offended. "Do you think it will serve?" he asked doubtfully.

"I think," Charles answered slowly, "that we all need encouragement at some time. Let her know how you feel about her and you may be surprised at the result."

~/~

The afternoon was one of ceaseless activity for Phoebe. But as she surveyed the ballroom that evening, she felt that it had all been worth the effort. The floor in the great hall had been scrubbed and polished to dangerously smooth perfection. The large chandelier blazed like a miniature constellation, illuminating the carved panels and rows of mirrors and gilt chairs along the eastern wall.

On the western wall, the spaces between the long French doors opening onto the terrace were filled with arrangements of vivid spring blossoms of every hue. Delightful!

Charles, coming up behind her, was also entranced by the scene before him. But it was not the room which brought that light into his eyes as his wife turned to greet him. Phoebe, standing framed in the doorway, was exquisitely beautiful. In a gown of Clarence-blue satin shimmering with silver spangles, her hair drawn back to cascade in artfully arranged curls over one bare shoulder, she was far too delectable for his peace of mind.

"Everything looks splendid, does it not?" she asked, taking the arm he offered and smiling at him bewitchingly.

"Splendid, indeed," he agreed. "But nothing surpasses you, my love."

"You like me in this gown?" she asked. "I was afraid you might think it too extravagant."

"Actually," he said, his color heightened ever so slightly, "my only thought was how much pleasure I should have removing it later tonight."

"If only this stupid ball were over!" she cried.

"Now, Phoebe," he chided gently, "you know there is nothing you enjoy so much as a ball."

She treated him to an impish look. "So I would have said once myself," she replied, only half teasing. "But I have recently discovered something I enjoy even more."

"Hussy!" he said, and would have kissed her there and then, had they not been joined at that moment by Letty and his mother.

Letitia was charming as always in a pure white dress with a single strand of pearls at her throat. Mrs. Hargood wore a gown of amaranthus color with a demi-train. An interesting turban perched on her head sported a tuft of small pink feathers, making her look like a curious but endearing bird.

Arriving just behind them, Olivia and Hortense were a sharp contrast. Olivia wore a hideous jonquille confection with an immoderate amount of flounces and bows and an assortment of mismatched jewels. Lady Chilton was dressed with perfect, if understated, taste in a plain green gown with puffed sleeves.

Lord Douglas was the last to arrive and immediately took advantage of his favored position by claiming as many dances with Letty as was decently allowed. After all, who could tell how many handsome young men would be present tonight to steal his thunder if he were not careful?

The sound of carriage wheels on the drive outside was the first sign that the other guests were beginning to arrive. Charles and Phoebe dutifully took their positions to greet them and spent the next hour or more in this tedious but obligatory exercise.

Sir John and Lady Northcote, and their son Harry had returned from a visit to Sir John's brother in Cambridge just in time to attend. They were among the first to make their entrance. Having last seen Phoebe at breakfast on that memorable day when Charles had announced his remarkable change of brides, they were eager to see how the couple were getting on.

Stephen and Emily Dodd, arriving shortly afterwards, were pleased to see their two friends so obviously happy. Phoebe was absolutely radiant, and Charles was more relaxed and sociable than they had ever seen him. A fine couple indeed.

Eventually, the last guest made his way up to

them, and Charles was pleased to introduce his octogenarian Great-uncle Andrew to Phoebe. Then Charles proudly led his lady to the center of the ballroom, where they officially opened the ball by dancing—of all things—a waltz. A rare treat, indeed, at a country ball.

By half past ten, it was clear that the Hargoods' ball was a resounding success. Young and old alike were equally impressed. It was, without question, the event of the season in this sleepy rural community, and was sure to be talked of for weeks to come. As it transpired, events were to make this particular ball one to be talked of for many years by all who attended.

The weather was unusually warm for the time of year, and Phoebe had had the forethought to have colored lanterns strung in the gardens around the terrace. Even the small fountain in the center of the terrace was skillfully illumined, giving a fairy-like aspect to the scene.

When the exertions of the dance proved a trifle too enervating, the heavily perspiring gentlemen and briskly fanning ladies were glad to quench their thirst with a little punch and to move outside in search of some revivifying fresh air. It was here, in a shadowed corner, that Charles at last found a brief moment to speak with Phoebe alone.

"Congratulations, my love," he said. "Your ball is a triumph."

"But of course! Did you ever doubt it? And remember," she added, "it is *our* ball."

Charles laughed, taking her hand in his and squeezing it affectionately. "I hope you do not over exert yourself," he said teasingly. "Emily is most concerned about you. She is convinced—to use the common phrase—that you are in a delicate condition. Perhaps," he went on, "she has been talking to Aunt Charlotte."

To his surprise, Phoebe did not even smile at

this sally. She stared at him so hard that he could not refrain from asking if anything were wrong.

"In another age," she informed him, "Emily Dodd would have been burned at the stake. She is too perceptive by half."

"Good God, Phoebe!" Charles exclaimed as the import of this speech penetrated. "You do not mean—?"

She looked a little apprehensive. "I had meant to tell you tonight," she admitted. "You do not mind, Charles?"

"Do *you* mind?" he asked in turn, eyeing her searchingly.

"How can you ask such a thing?" she cried, a little hurt by his question. "I love you, Charles! Do you not know how much it means to me that I will be the mother of your children?"

His grip on her hand tightened painfully. "Phoebe," he whispered. "My dearest love. If only you knew how happy you have made me. If only I could find the words to tell you how I feel—"

Looking up, Phoebe caught the look of naked adoration in his warm, dark eyes, and her last lingering doubt vanished. "Later," she told him, smiling, "you may tell me as much as you like—and show me too, if you wish."

Charles groaned. "You should not say such things, Phoebe! It is hard enough for me to keep from kissing you as it is."

"The last thing I want to do," she said, holding the back of his hand against her warm cheek, "is to keep you from kissing me. Oh Charles," she continued, suddenly serious, "I'm afraid I shall be the most jealous and possessive of wives! Every woman over sixteen and under sixty will be my sworn enemy. And I shall want you to be making love to me all the time."

Though the words were spoken half in jest, Charles knew how badly Phoebe's confidence had suffered from Robert's unfaithfulness. "Be as jealous as you choose," he replied, turning his hand to tenderly stroke her cheek. "It will be my pleasure to prove to you, every day, that there is only one woman I desire—and that is you, my dearest wife."

"You are the most wonderful husband, the most perfect lover, and the most amazing man in the world. I would say more," Phoebe whispered, "but at the moment I believe Letty is about to descend upon us."

Her prediction was instantly fulfilled as Letty came running up to them, crying, "Oh Phoebe! I have the most wonderful news. I am to be married!"

Phoebe, looking at the beaming countenance of Douglas, who was standing behind her jubilant friend, said, "What! Has Douglas finally gotten up the courage to offer for you?"

Letty was all amazement. "Did you know, then, that he loved me? And would tell me nothing? How cruel!"

"But Letty," Phoebe asked playfully, "what of your recent disappointment over Henry Fernleigh?"

Letty dismissed her former idol with a careless shrug. "I suppose you will never let me forget that childish infatuation," she said airily. "But I have known for weeks that I was in love with Douglas. And when I think how you must have deliberately led me to believe he was in love with you —"

Phoebe, however, would have none of this. "That was entirely your own idea. I merely encouraged it."

"This is a night of wonders, indeed," Charles interposed lest Phoebe's high spirits should lead her into too much mischief. "Let me congratulate you, Ardshire," he said, shaking the other's hand vigorously.

"It was you who gave me the push I needed to come up to scratch tonight," Douglas admitted. He then had to recount to the two women what Charles had advised him to do.

Letty at once perceived that Charles must be her guardian angel, and Phoebe was quite overcome. "So!" she declared, "after all my efforts on your behalf, Douglas, you owe your success to Charles. This is almost too much for me!"

"I think," Letty said to Phoebe in some surprise, "that there is more romance in Charles than you have given him credit for. Somehow, it does not seem at all strange that you should love him now."

"To me, it is the most natural thing in the world," Phoebe answered, very much in earnest.

"I am happy that things have come about so well for us all," Charles said, looking lovingly at his wife.

"Indeed," said Phoebe, "if we could but rid ourselves of Olivia and Hortense, we should have nothing left to wish for."

The words were scarcely out of Phoebe's mouth when a loud screech from the other side of the terrace claimed everyone's attention. Apparently a large moth—confused, no doubt, by the lanterns in the garden and the bright light blazing out of the open windows—had blundered unwisely amongst the guests outside. The unfortunate creature chose the bodice of Miss Loftbury's gown as a temporary resting place.

Eyeing the monstrous insect in utter horror, Olivia took strong exception to its presence upon her person. Had she merely swooned, as any gently-bred lady should, all would have ended with a minimum of bother. Instead, she succumbed to a fit of the most violent hysterics. Waving her arms about wildly and screaming at the top of her lungs, she galloped blindly through the crowd in a misguided attempt to escape her winged attacker.

As Charles, Phoebe, and the assembled company looked on in helpless astonishment, Miss Loftbury concluded her mad dash by cannoning directly into Lady Chilton. Hortense, quite unprepared, staggered back and lost her balance.

Unfortunately, at that precise moment she was standing beside the fountain. Before anyone could lift a finger to stop them, the inexorable law of gravity had its inevitable effect: the two women tumbled together into the water with the most spectacular splash.

Never at any ball had anyone witnessed such a grand entertainment! It was far better than fireworks. Why, Sadler's Wells could produce no aquatic performance to compare with this! As Phoebe and Charles hurried to rescue the two sodden ladies, they were aware of more than one hastily stifled titter. Olivia, all unwittingly, had provided the crowning achievement to a most unusual evening.

Charles assisted his dripping sister out of the water while Douglas did the same for Miss Loftbury. Phoebe led them into the house, Olivia weeping copiously and Hortense looking at the author of her misfortune with intense loathing. Phoebe wondered if their friendship would survive this disaster. By the exertion of supreme self-will, she managed to refrain from laughter and tried to do what she could for them both, though neither seemed especially grateful for her solicitude.

Hortense and Olivia could not doubt that the unfortunate incident would be discussed with great glee by everyone who had witnessed their horribly public disgrace. Their humiliation was complete, and most appropriate. Both expressed their resolute intention of departing the very next day, and their host and hostess kindly refrained from pressing them to remain.

Taking her daughter's ill luck in very good part, Mrs. Hargood declared, "I do not know when I have enjoyed an evening more!"

It was a sentiment shared by all who were privileged to have been there that memorable night—including Charles and Phoebe Hargood. The last impediment to their comfort and tranquillity was now, miraculously, removed.

Chapter Sixteen

As they made their way from Boodle's, Charles and Douglas strolled companionably along St. James's Street, occasionally stopping to greet an acquaintance. Douglas was holding forth on the merits of a new curricle he had recently purchased.

"Letty is mad to drive it, of course."

"Naturally." Charles nodded in understanding. "Though I trust she will not attempt it in her present condition."

"If I were fool enough to allow her," he confessed. "But she has promised not to venture near it for the next seven months."

"That must have taken considerable persuasion on your part."

Douglas shuddered. "I had to promise her that I'd teach her, myself, to handle the reins."

"I suspected as much." Charles chuckled and shook his head. "I wish you luck, sir."

"I have no doubt I shall need it. Letty is so high-strung. You should have seen her when we went to Week's Mechanical Museum this Monday past!"

Apparently, Letty had insisted on visiting this attraction, located in Haymarket. At first she had been quite delighted with it, eyeing the various clocks and other curiosities with considerable interest. The mechanical tarantula, however, was another matter entirely. One look at its menacing movements had brought about a sudden revulsion and the command to remove her from the building at once! Her husband had not hesitated to comply, since she was looking rather pale.

"I thought you would have had more sense than to take her there," Charles scolded him. "Under the circumstances, you may count yourself fortunate that she did not swoon. It would not have been the first time."

"Thank God she did not," Douglas agreed. "I do not know what I should have done. I have not yet had to witness such a calamity."

"Well I have."

"On a certain unforgettable morning at Camberley?"

They reached a busy street corner and carefully made their way across before Charles responded. He and Douglas were on the best of terms these days, while their wives remained close friends. It was partly because of Letty that the Hargoods were in town again, for she had recently discovered that she was increasing, as the vulgar phrased it. She wanted Phoebe's company and support during the most trying weeks, for she was feeling very poorly. The past week had seen a lessening of her symptoms, however, and Phoebe and Charles intended to return to Camberley on the morrow.

"Her entrance that morning," Charles said, having gained the opposite side of the street, "was certainly a marvelous spectacle."

Douglas tipped his hat to an elderly gentleman who hailed them as they passed. "No doubt she thought you and Phoebe a spectacle as well."

"So we were. And I, for one, was not pleased at Letty's unexpected intrusion." He smiled, reminiscing. "But I can hardly bear her any ill will, seeing that the ultimate result has been so fortuitous."

"Indeed. Phoebe is positively blooming."

"She is glad to be in London again," Charles acknowledged with a slight frown. "The shops, as you, and my pocketbook know, all too well!"

"It is very good to have you both here again," Douglas responded. They turned another corner and found themselves on the sunny side of the street. "We cannot always be visiting you in the country, after all."

"I ought to have brought her to town before, perhaps."

"Perhaps." Douglas shrugged.

"It is full four months since Anthony was born. The season is all but over."

"I do not think that signifies to Phoebe."

"I hope you are right."

A few more minutes brought them to the door of the London house. Going inside, they were met by Mrs. Hargood, who informed them that Phoebe and Letty had not yet returned from their shopping expedition.

Douglas quipped that they would probably exhaust the last of their pin money. His resources were dwindling daily, he claimed, and he only prayed he would not find himself rolled up by summer's end.

Neither Charles nor his mother heeded such outrageous hyperbole.

Douglas was far too well-heeled to be in financial straits. But Charles was a little concerned by the absence of the two ladies, especially when another hour passed without any sign of them. Surely they should have returned by this time? What could possibly be keeping them?

~/~

Phoebe and Letitia were, in fact, enjoying a wonderful romp through the linen-drapers, milliners and corsetiers of Mayfair and Leicester Square.

They had already plundered Grafton House, where Phoebe had purchased several yards of exquisite capucine-colored silk, which she intended for a dinner dress in a style she had recently seen in *La Belle Assemblée*. Letty had agreed that the dark orange color would complement her lustrous dark hair. In addition, she must have a muslin walking dress and a theatre dress, for she and Charles were considering a brief stay in Bath, perhaps in September. Letty was all enthusiasm, helping her friend to choose colors and styles. She even made a few purchases herself, though she said she had less need to replenish her wardrobe, as she and Douglas spent more time in the city than the Hargoods did.

The two women had made their way to a fashionable milliner and were debating the merits of a gypsy hat of chipped straw and a poke bonnet, trying to decide which would be more practical before buying both of them. Phoebe examined the brim of the bonnet, pursing her lips as she pondered whether Charles would find it attractive, and how it would enhance her features. Would it do for an afternoon stroll, perhaps?

Suddenly she felt Letty's fingers squeeze her upper arm with what seemed to be unnecessary force.

"What is wrong, Letty?"

"Over by the door," Letty whispered. "No! Don't look," she added, as Phoebe's head automatically began to turn in that direction.

"But what is it?" Phoebe demanded. "If I am not to look, you must certainly tell me."

"Clarissa!"

"Lady Stainford?"

For a moment, Phoebe felt a faint prickle of something like fear run through her. It was more than a year since her last encounter with the redhead, but she could hardly be expected to forget such a conversation as they had shared when Clarissa convinced her that Charles was an unfaithful husband. Phoebe was reluctant even to look at her old nemesis. But surely it was foolish to be so apprehensive. What harm could the creature do to her now?

She raised her head from the bonnet she was holding, and her gaze immediately encountered that of the other woman.

Clarissa spoke first. "Why, if it is not Mrs. Hargood!" she exclaimed. "What a happy coincidence."

"Is it not?" Phoebe schooled herself not to hiss at her.

"And Miss Comston…oh, I beg your pardon!" Clarissa laughed. "It is Lady Ardshire now, I believe."

"Good afternoon, ma'am," Letty said, adopting a stiff politeness intended to depress any pretension. "How do you do?"

Phoebe could scarcely suppress a smile at her friend's newfound toploftiness. Her position as Douglas's wife was teaching her a new maturity, which included the ability to give a set-down in the most charming manner.

"Oh, I am always well," Clarissa informed them, feigning indifference, though Phoebe noticed her color heightened ever so slightly. "I hope you are not contemplating the purchase of that dreadful hat, Phoebe. But then, you are so seldom in town these days that one cannot wonder at your ignorance of current fashion."

"You are right, my dear Clarissa," Phoebe said, matching smile for smile. "I am sadly *démodé*. That is why I brought Letitia along to advise me what best to buy, that I might not look an absolute frump."

"I daresay it will not matter if you do." Clarissa shrugged a pale shoulder. "Your country friends will hardly notice any difference."

Clarissa's obvious efforts to quiz and insult her

should have made Phoebe very angry. But she was surprised to feel nothing more than a mild amusement. It no longer mattered what this woman might say or do. Charles had never really cared for Clarissa. Her liaison with him had been nothing more than a foolish fancy bred by Phoebe's own irrational jealousy. With something like shock, she suddenly realized that this woman truly had no power over her. The shoe was very much on the other foot now, for Phoebe was secure in the love of her husband, and she felt a sense of strength and certainty which shielded her from every dart Clarissa might aim.

"One takes a different view of things in the country," Phoebe said, smiling.

"It must be terribly dull for you, my dear."

"Quite the contrary." Phoebe laid aside the bonnet and reached for the gypsy hat. "Were it not for Charles, I suppose it would be difficult to accustom myself to it. But I have discovered that, so long as he is with me, I can find pleasure in most things."

"But he cannot be with you all the time, can he?"

"We spend every possible moment together," Phoebe assured her, "although Charles often declares that he wishes it were more."

"Do you not pine for town life after all this rustication?"

"Not at all." Phoebe's smile widened at the thought. "Charles has taught me to appreciate country life. There is nothing to tempt him to come to town very often, after all. And I would be quite miserable here without him."

There was a hard, angry look in Clarissa's eyes. "How quaint," she said. "I only hope the novelty may not wear off too soon."

"I think there is little chance of that," Letty put in at this point. "Charles and Phoebe are very much in love."

"Indeed?" Clarissa gave a short, sharp laugh. "Love matches seem to be all the rage these days. For myself, I find love to be far less reliable than money as a means of providing happiness."

"Letty and I," Phoebe said gently, "are very fortunate to have both."

"Love and country living seem to agree with you, Phoebe." Clarissa examined her figure from head to toe. "You are rather more plump than I remember."

This new piece of malice completely missed its mark. Phoebe was well aware that she was not quite so slender as she had been, but she was not obese by any means. Her few additional pounds had certainly not decreased Charles's appetite for lovemaking. If anything, he was more demanding than ever—which she did not object to in the least.

"The plumpness I must blame on my son, I suppose." Phoebe looked directly into Clarissa's cold blue eyes. "But his father does not seem to mind. Indeed, if I mistake not, he is quite eager to provide little Anthony with a brother or sister."

"What? Another squealing infant? That should not suit me at all." Clarissa did not trouble to hide her scorn.

"I find that it suits me remarkably well."

"I suppose one must resign oneself, at any rate. You have chosen your lot in life, and there is no use repining over what cannot be changed, is there?"

"I would not change my situation for anything in the world."

"Bravely spoken!" Clarissa treated the whole thing as a jest. "But I doubt not that there are times you yearn for the pleasures you left behind in the city, however earnestly you may deny it."

Phoebe treated Clarissa to a pitying look. "I only wish that I could explain to you all that I have learned about pleasure since my marriage to Charles. But I fear that you would not understand what I am talking about, since you have plainly not experienced anything like it yourself."

Clarissa's eyes narrowed, but she did not pursue the subject. Instead, she launched into a lively description of a recent ball held at the London residence of Alastair Garvine, a wealthy widower of some sixty years. While his fortune was undoubtedly derived from trade, Mr. Garvine had managed to gain entree into certain more exalted circles for obvious reasons. The highest sticklers might snub him; however, those whose titles were grand but whose pockets were no longer plump, were eager enough to court his favor.

"Mr. Garvine is your particular friend, is he?" Letty asked, not quite managing to conceal her distaste.

"La! How do you expect me to answer that?" Clarissa protested, glancing up slyly from beneath the wide brim of her hat. "A lady must not be too sure of her conquests, must she?"

"No, indeed. Not," Phoebe added, unable to resist, "that Mr. Garvine would be a conquest of which I would choose to boast. A bit long in the tooth, and not very tonnish. But, I suppose, a woman of your age cannot afford to be too particular."

Several patrons of Madame Arnaud's establishment had been straining to catch the conversation between the two women, and at this point a pregnant hush fell upon the room.

Even Letty seemed to be holding her breath. Would Clarissa recover from this doubler?

"Mr. Garvine," she said, drawing herself up stiffly and fixing a venomous stare on her opponent, "is a most respectable man. And," she added with emphasis, "it is well known that he is rich enough to buy an Abbey!"

"In that case," said Phoebe, "I wish you every imaginable success. After all, I always thought you had the makings of a capital abbess."

Clarissa drew in a shuddering breath. But before she could respond, Phoebe had turned away and called for Madam Arnaud herself, having made her selection. Clarissa was left standing alone, her cheeks an unbecoming shade of red, while several interested ladies looked on in quiet satisfaction. Few women had ever been so deserving of such an insult. When the offended lady swept from the establishment a few moments later, nobody felt the least regret at her departure, and everyone was eager to quit the place as well, in order to spread this latest *on-dit*, which was far too delicious to keep to oneself.

~/~

The two ladies returned home in high spirits. While the servants hauled her purchases up to her room to be packed away for tomorrow's journey, Phoebe led a laughing Letitia into the drawing room where their husbands awaited them.

"Where have you been, my sweet?" Douglas inquired, eyeing his wife with some concern. "I hope you have not been overexerting yourself. Charles and I were becoming quite worried."

"That is most gratifying," Phoebe answered, moving to link arms with her husband. "But quite unnecessary."

"You seem to be in fine fettle, indeed," Charles agreed.

"I do not know when I have ever enjoyed anything so much," Letty informed the two men. "Phoebe was wonderful!"

Charles smiled fondly at his wife. "Phoebe is always wonderful."

"But today," Letty declared with simple conviction, "she has outdone herself."

"One hardly dares ask," Charles said to his wife, "what you have been doing."

"Nothing too shocking, I trust?" Douglas quizzed her.

"Certainly not!" Letty protested. "I only wish your mother had been there, Charles. She would have appreciated it, I know."

"Then you must certainly tell her all about it when she returns from visiting her friend."

"But what happened?" Douglas insisted.

Phoebe lowered her lashes demurely. "If you will have a full account, you must hear it from your wife, Douglas."

Letty needed no further prompting. She launched into the tale of their encounter with Lady Stainford with unalloyed enthusiasm. From their chance meeting, through her unsuccessful attempts to bait Phoebe, to the dramatic *dénouement*, she painted so vivid a portrait of the scene that the gentlemen had no difficulty imagining its development. Concluding with Phoebe's crushing remark, it was no wonder that her listeners were momentarily rendered speechless.

"Phoebe!" Douglas gasped at last. "You never said such a thing! You could not."

"I thought you knew her better than that, Ardshire," Charles corrected him. "It is no arduous task for me to believe it."

"There were several ladies present who overheard us, I am sure," Phoebe said. "I can provide you with their names, if you wish for confirmation, Douglas."

"I thought several of them were about to cheer," Letty added.

"You are not angry with me, Charles?" Phoebe asked with sudden misgiving. "I know I promised not to do anything too scandalous."

"On the contrary, my love." Charles's arm

tightened about her shoulders. "I am very proud of my intrepid wife. Clarissa was long overdue for a helping of humiliation. I can never forget that, but for her malice, we would both have been spared a good deal of heartache. I only regret that I was not present to witness her defeat at your very capable hands."

"I think I can see her face even now." Letty's heartfelt sigh was accompanied by a look of purest satisfaction.

This was too much for her husband, who began to chuckle softly. In a moment, the chuckle grew to a full-throated laugh, which proved so irresistible that they were soon all convulsed with mirth—so much so, that more than one curious servant peeped around the door to witness a spectacle of such unseemly vulgarity.

Eventually they managed to control their emotions, and Douglas was able to say, "Phoebe, you are better than a tonic! I do not know what we shall do without you."

"I shall miss you terribly," Letty agreed, sobering.

"You shall be visiting us at Camberley within a fortnight," Charles reminded her.

"I am sure you will be able to survive without me for that long." Phoebe wiped her still moist eyes.

"Do not be so sure." Charles was only half in jest. "I think you do not realize how hard it is to be separated from you. I can attest that it is a most painful experience indeed."

"It is an experience you will not often have to endure, my love," she assured him. "That I promise you."

Epilogue

It was wonderful to be home again—home at Camberley. Not at all fatigued from their brief journey, Phoebe and Charles dined with the squire and his lady. Mrs. Hargood, who accompanied them, could not forbear to relate the tale of Clarissa's defeat, which both Stepehen and Emily Dodd found every bit as entertaining as she had expected.

Mrs. Hargood had now returned to the dower house, and Phoebe and Charles prepared to retire for the night.. The dull green decor of Charles's bedchamber had been replaced by a brighter motif in shades of blue and gold. Charles was already in bed when Phoebe entered.

Though they had shared this room for more than a year now, he still felt a thrill of pleasurable anticipation as he watched his wife begin to remove her robe.

"Has Anthony quieted down for the night?" he asked.

"Your son," she replied, slipping beneath the covers beside him, "has finally deigned to go to sleep. I have left him to the care of Mrs. Delford, who will call me if I am needed."

Charles turned fully on his side to look more closely at his wife. How lovely she was, he thought for the thousandth time. How undeservedly fortunate he was to have her. Was she happy here with him? he wondered. She seemed content, but her life was very different from what it had been before.

"Do you mind that we left London so soon?" he asked with sudden concern. "I do not want you to feel confined here at Camberley, Phoebe. I know how much you enjoy town life."

Phoebe smiled at this. Surely Charles must know how happy he had made her. What did it matter if they spent little time in London? The amusements of fashionable life were too often a pathetic attempt to fill empty and meaningless lives with enough noise and folly to drown the silence within. Her life was full, her cup overflowing.

She had sympathetic and warm friends around her, a beautiful baby boy to cherish, and a husband who loved her as few women had ever been loved. She would be a monster of ingratitude, indeed, if she did not thank God each day for such blessings.

"Letty and Douglas will be coming down very soon," she said at last. "That will make a pleasant change."

"Douglas and Letitia are always here," Charles countered, not to be deterred. "But what of us, Phoebe? Shall we go to Paris? Would you like that, my love?"

She cupped his face in her hands, pressing a quick kiss upon his lips. "Certainly," she answered him. "I should be happy to visit Paris, or Brussels, or Madrid, or Bury Saint Edmunds. My happiness depends not on where I may be, but with whom."

"You do not find it dull here?" He was still anxious.

Her eyes opened very wide. "With *you* here?" she returned. "Remember the day we went riding together and found that little clearing in the woods?"

Charles wagged his finger at her accusingly. "Your conduct that afternoon was scandalous. What if someone had discovered us?"

"You were the one who chose that spot to stop for a short time!" she cried, quite indignant. "I merely suggested that there were other things we might do there than to eat lunch—and I did not notice you refusing my suggestion."

"It was a most enjoyable day," he admitted with a grin.

"Precisely!" she agreed. "So why go to Paris? We can have just as pleasant a time here. And think of the money we save!"

Charles laughed outright. "Mistress Economy," he teased.

"I have always been most economical," she protested. "Just think, Charles! Most women require two men to please them: a husband and a lover. But I have married a man who can do the work of both."

"Do you remember the first time we shared this bed?" he asked, casting a look about the room.

"How could I forget? It was the luckiest day of my life."

"Would you be good enough to inform me, madam," Charles said with mock severity, "what you are doing in my bed?"

But this time Phoebe's response was quite different. She moved even closer to him, sliding her arms around his neck and looking boldly into his eyes. "What am I doing here?" she asked him. "A most impertinent question, if I may say so, sir. But, if you must know, I have a perfectly reasonable excuse. I," she breathed into his ear, "am about to pleasure my husband. What have you to say to that?"

Charles turned his head until his lips were a mere whisper away from hers. "If that is the case, ma'am," he said, "you may stay. In fact, I insist upon it!"

The End

Regency Press == Order Form

☐ **A Regency Sampler**
August, 1999 #1-929085-00-1 / $5.95

☐ **The Marplot Marriage by Beth Andrews**
October, 1999 #1-929085-01-X / $4.95

☐ **The Reluctant Guardian by Jo Manning**
December, 1999 #1-929085-06-0 / $4.95

Prices slightly higher outside the U.S. Payable in U.S. funds only. No cash/COD accepted. Postage & handling: U.S./CAN. $3.00 for one book, $1.50 for each additional book, total not to exceed $10.00. International orders: $6.00 for first book, $2.00 for each additional. We accept VISA, MasterCard, AMEX or Discover/Novus ($10.00 minimum); checks ($25.00 fee for returned checks) and money orders, made payable to: Regency Press. Call/fax (216) 932-5319 or 1-87REGENCY9. (877-343-6299). Or visit our web-site: **http://www.regency-press.com** Please allow 4-6 weeks for delivery; foreign and Canadian delivery 6-8 weeks.

Regency Press Bill my: ☐ VISA ☐ MasterCard
P. O. Box 18908 Card # ____________________
Cleveland Hts OH 44118-0908 Exp. Date __________
Signature: ____________________
SHIP TO:
Name: ____________________
Address: ____________________
City: ____________________
State/Zip: ____________________
Telephone: ____________________
Book Total: ____________________
Sales Tax: ____________________ (7% in Ohio)
Postage : ____________________
Total Due/Enclosed: ____________________